Three O'Clock in the Morning

A NOVEL

Gianrico Carofiglio

Translated from the Italian by Howard Curtis

HARPERVIA

An Imprint of HarperCollins*Publishers*

HarperCollins books may be purchased for educational, business, or sales promotional use. For information, please email the Special Markets Department at SPsales@harpercollins.com.

Originally published as *Le tre del mattino* in Italy in 2017 by Giulio Einaudi editore.

First published in English in Australia in 2021 by Text Publishing.

First HarperVia edition published 2021.

Translation copyright © 2021 by Howard Curtis.

FIRST EDITION

Designed by SBI Book Arts, LLC

Library of Congress Cataloging-in-Publication Data

Names: Carofiglio, Gianrico, 1961– author. | Curtis, Howard, 1949– translator.
Title: Three o'clock in the morning / by Gianrico Carofiglio ; translated from the Italian by Howard Curtis.
Other titles: Tre del mattino. English
Description: First edition. | New York, NY : HarperVia, 2021. | Originally published as Le tre del mattino in Italy in 2017 by Giulio Einaudi editore.
Identifiers: LCCN 2020021756 | ISBN 9780063028449 (hardcover) | ISBN 9780063028470 (trade paperback) | ISBN 9780063028456 (ebook) | ISBN 9780063028463
Classification: LCC PQ4903.A665 T7413 2021 | DDC 853/.92—dc23
LC record available at https://lccn.loc.gov/2020021756

21 22 23 24 25   LSC   10 9 8 7 6 5 4 3 2 1

Three O'Clock in the Morning

London Borough of Hackney	
91300001145292	
Askews & Holts	
AF	£20.00
	6491903

I

I can't say when it started. Maybe I was seven, maybe a little older, I don't remember exactly. When you're a child, it's not clear to you what's normal and what isn't. Come to think of it, it's not all that clear when you're an adult either.

About once a month, something strange and rather distressing would happen to me. Without warning, I would notice an absence, a feeling of detachment from the world around me, yet at the same time, my senses would become more acute.

Usually, we select the stimuli that come to us from the outside world. We are surrounded by sounds, smells, all kinds of visible entities. But we aren't objective; we don't hear everything that bounces off our eardrums, we don't smell everything that reaches our nose, we don't see everything that hits our retinas. The brain decides which perceptions to become aware of, which information to register.

All the rest stays out; we are accustomed to excluding details, and yet it's all there. If we wanted to notice all of it, we could.

Stop reading and concentrate on the noises around you,

the noises you weren't conscious of until a few seconds ago. You may be in a quiet room, but you'll still detect the sound of some distant equipment, a rustling, a humming, voices—some close, some farther away—whose words you can't make out but are there. And you'll become aware of the movements, the vibrations produced by your body: your breathing, your heartbeat, the gurgling of your digestive system.

It may not be a pleasant sensation. For me, it certainly wasn't. Now I know that during these episodes my brain stopped making selections and just let everything in. For a few minutes, I would be unable to speak, and I would just sit there, as if I were drunk.

For years, I never told anybody about it. I thought it was just a normal part of the way I was, and besides, I wouldn't have known what to say. I didn't have the words to describe the experiences.

Then one day I happened to be in the home of a classmate of mine, Ernesto, the son of an officer in the Carabinieri who lived in a vast service apartment. We were playing Subbuteo in the dining room, having just eaten toffees—God knows why I remember that detail.

His mother was sitting in an armchair. I think she was knitting.

I was just about to score a goal and suddenly, with a violence I had never experienced before, I was assaulted by a terrible cacophony of noise that arrived like a river in full flood, swollen with debris. The impact was so powerful that, for a few seconds, I lost consciousness.

I came to in an armchair, the same one where Ernesto's

mother had previously been sitting. She was leaning over me, stroking my face, and speaking in a worried tone.

"Antonio, Antonio, how do you feel?"

"Fine," I replied, tentatively.

"What happened to you?"

"What happened to me?"

"You weren't speaking, and it seemed like you couldn't hear. Then you fainted."

The noise had gone, but I was still confused and couldn't say anything. Then Ernesto's mother called my mother and told her what had happened. When I got home, I was subjected to another interrogation.

"What happened to you, Antonio?"

"I don't know. I mean, nothing strange."

"Ernesto's mom says they were speaking to you and you weren't answering, as if you were dazed or asleep."

"It happens sometimes."

"What do you mean, it happens?"

I made an effort to describe the thing that occasionally happened to me and which appeared in a more aggressive form that afternoon.

The feeling that someone was playing a drum in my chest. My breathing, so heavy as to convince me that if I got distracted, if I stopped thinking about breathing, I would choke to death.

The most ordinary sounds transformed into a tangled din.

And on top of that, there was another thing that happened to me with some frequency: the impression that I'd already lived through the moment I was currently experiencing. Before

3

long, I would be told that it was called déjà vu and was a relatively common phenomenon. But back then, I didn't know that, and there were times when I felt as if I were living in a world of ghosts.

My mother called my father, and half an hour later he joined us. This made me think the problem was quite serious and that perhaps I had underestimated my symptoms. My parents had separated when I was nine and since then Dad had come to Mom's apartment—which had previously also been his apartment—only a very few times, and never in the evening. Whenever I went to his place, he'd come to pick me up, I'd go downstairs, get in his car and we'd leave.

He asked me the same questions and I think I gave him the same answers. After which they called Dr. Placidi, our family doctor. He was an elderly, friendly gentleman with a big white moustache, broken capillaries on his nose and a sickly sweet smell on his breath that I was only able to identify many years later. I don't know if my parents were aware that our faithful doctor wasn't exactly a teetotaler.

He came to our apartment and examined me, but mainly asked me lots of questions. Did I have convulsions? He explained what they were, and I said no, I'd never had them. Did I have colorful hallucinations or moments of total darkness? No, not those either.

All I had were these periods of sensory overload, during which I remained conscious and was still able to orient myself, although with difficulty.

That afternoon at Ernesto's, everything had been more intense. Still basically, it didn't seem too different from when

I became distracted at school, stopped listening to what the teachers were saying and started fantasizing.

"Do you ever get distracted at school?" the doctor said.

"Sometimes."

"As if you don't hear what the teachers are saying to you?"

I glanced at my mother and father. I wasn't sure I should share that kind of information with them, but then I decided it was important to cooperate with the doctor and nodded. He smiled in approval, as if I'd given the correct answer. The smell of his breath was a little stronger than usual.

He made me do strange exercises. I had to balance on one leg, close my eyes and touch the tip of my nose, first with my right index finger, then with my left index finger; take hold of one of his thumbs and squeeze it hard.

"Nothing to worry about," he said, at last, addressing my father. "It's a normal neuro-vegetative disorder. It happens to children, especially the more sensitive ones. When he's in his teens, these phenomena will disappear." Then he turned to me and added, "Your brain is electrically overactive, it's a sign of intelligence."

Neuro-vegetative disorder was a vague diagnosis. It could mean anything or nothing. Like going to your doctor to complain about a headache and he examines you and tells you you have a headache.

But Dr. Placidi had a reassuring manner, a reassuring way of speaking—apart from his breath—so my parents were duly reassured. Life resumed its regular course; what happened that afternoon was quickly forgotten.

2

The years passed, fairly normally.

Despite the somewhat approximate diagnosis, the doctor's prediction was turning out to be accurate.

Now it only happened once a month, and the sensations were increasingly tenuous and indefinite. The only worrying thing was the déjà vu, with its aura of a vaguely supernatural phenomenon.

Basically, it was a thing of moments, and I was about to file it all away, like when you empty the wardrobes and shelves of your childhood room and put away forever the exercise books with the big squares, the textbooks, the smock and bow of your elementary school uniform, the boxes of toy soldiers and animals and cars.

I was in my first year of high school and had just gotten home from school. My mother, too, had just come home from the university. She was making something for lunch or talking on the phone; I'm not sure which.

I was in my room, sitting in the rocking chair, reading a cowboy comic book.

After a while, the doors and windows shook—because of the wind, I thought. The noise was so loud that I suspected an earthquake. I got up cautiously and was hit by a deluge of sounds: the TV in the next room, a moped in the street, my racing heart, my labored breathing that sounded like something out of an underwater documentary or a suspense movie, even my few unsteady steps on the floor.

I had a light blue bedspread, almost sky blue. All at once, that pale, relaxing color grew threatening, it came to life, leaped toward me like some psychedelic entity, and went right through me with an unreal violence. Immediately after, a beam of light emanated from that same bedspread, a kind of rainbow, first light blue, then dark blue, yellow, and other colors, until it became a blinding white that turned into a series of luminous streaks. These intersected, joined, divided and multiplied, gradually filling my field of vision.

The din became deafening. I covered my ears with my hands and tried to cry for help. I don't know if I succeeded, because it's the last thing I remember.

Some years later, Mom would tell me she had found me on the floor, unconscious but shaking convulsively, my eyes rolled back.

In my personal film of the episode, that fade-out is followed by a subjective shot from a hospital bed: a room with furniture the color of condensed milk.

There were people around me, but at that moment nobody was looking at me. My mother and father were there, along with some men in white coats. They were talking among themselves in low voices. Then someone noticed that I had woken up.

My parents came over to me.

"Antonio, how are you feeling?" my mother said, taking my hand and stroking my forehead. An uncommon gesture from her, and one that made me feel like crying.

"What happened?" I asked after a moment or two.

"You . . . you had a turn, a very strong dizzy spell . . ." There was something strange in her tone. Mom usually spoke in a precise, confident way, in complete sentences, as if reading from a well-written script. Not this time.

"You had a turn," my father echoed. "But don't worry, we're in the hospital now. The doctors have to run a few tests, and then you'll be home in no time at all."

Even in my Valium-induced state, the discrepancy between my father's reassuring words and his expression was very clear to me. He seemed like a little boy suddenly informed of the true nature of the world and its mortal dangers.

He was joined by one of the men in white coats. He had a dark complexion, five o'clock shadow up his cheeks, and a low hairline. He asked me how I was feeling now, what I'd felt before I lost consciousness, and other things that weren't completely clear to me.

I felt drowsy; it was as if I had woken up for a few moments to look around me but wanted to go back to sleep right away.

My memory of what happened in the next few days is also confused.

Things certainly didn't go the way my father had promised. They didn't take me home immediately. I stayed in the hospital for quite a long time, more than a week.

During those days, I lost all sense of time. Morning, evening, and night merged into one, what with my constant drowsiness and my restless sleep, while men and women in white came and examined me, took blood, gave me injections and administered all kinds of pills and drops.

Sometimes I was taken to a room full of antiquated, fearsome-looking equipment. There, I would have electrodes attached to my head and be made to do balance exercises while the printouts emerging from the machine were examined with a bored air.

I was taken back to my room. I threw myself on the bed and stayed there, vegetating, never getting up. I didn't want to do anything, not even read the books and comics brought by my parents or the relatives who came to see me, looking sheepish and feigning flippancy. I shared a room with another boy who was in worse shape than me. He, too, was always in bed, with a drip in his arm, completely absent. The only person who came to see him was his mother, a prematurely aged, gray-looking woman in whose eyes I occasionally caught flashes of sullen resentment.

I had two more attacks, much less strong than the last one, and learned the name of my illness—idiopathic generalized epilepsy—which means: the kind of epilepsy the doctors can't identify the cause of. At best, they make more or less reasonable conjectures. My epilepsy *might* be due to a trauma that had occurred during birth, or there *might* be other causes, causes they *might* never discover.

Based on this not very reassuring premise, the doctors developed a complex therapeutic plan and decided they could discharge me.

The worst was about to begin.

3

In my memory, there is a monotonous continuity between the days spent in the hospital, in bed, without energy, without any desire to do anything, and the days spent at home, in bed, without energy, without any desire to do anything.

When I was discharged, the neurologists handed us several pages of prescriptions. I had to take four tablets a day—the anti-convulsant, vitamins, the other anti-convulsant, and a fourth drug—each at a different time; this alone made life complicated enough.

The real problem, though, wasn't the medicines. One of those papers was a list of rules that had to be strictly observed. They were varied, and—thinking of them with hindsight—all absurd.

Avoid places that were too crowded, particularly those "with high noise thresholds"; abstain from contact sports, including soccer; go to bed early, sleep nine hours a night, avoid coffee and any other alkaloids or stimulants: lead a regular life.

In addition, I had to eliminate fizzy drinks, including mineral water.

Fizzy drinks. Consuming them—the consultant had explained to my parents, who had immediately been dubious as to the scientific basis of this strange edict—might cause some kind of reaction, which in turn might set off a new epileptic seizure.

That was it. The real problem was those words, their unpleasant sound, their shameful feel.

Epileptic seizure. Epilepsy.

I was an epileptic. An unspeakable condition, which somehow suggested mental illness and which would be better to keep hidden.

I sensed this while I was in the hospital, and it became even clearer to me when I was due to go back to school, and my mother made a strangely awkward speech.

"So—back to school tomorrow. You must be pleased."

I wasn't. I was apathetic. Every little thing seemed blurred, both inside and outside me. I shrugged half-heartedly. I wasn't making her task any easier.

"I'll go with you," she went on. "That way, I can take the medical certificate with me and show them all that everything's fine."

Everything's fine?

"The certificate says that you had a concussion following a fall, you were admitted to the hospital for tests, and everything's fine now."

It was an assertion on her part, but the tone was hesitant, almost questioning, as if she were putting forward a hypothesis or a work plan and asking for my approval.

"As the doctor explained, this . . . *condition* of yours may right itself, or rather, it definitely will right itself in a few years, taking the medicines and all the rest. But it really isn't necessary to go into detail about what happened."

She looked at me to see if I was following her. I was. My mother had put into words my first, vague notion: I had a shameful illness, and it would be better to keep it hidden.

"Kids—adults too, to tell the truth—can be very stupid. They attach labels to a person just because he has a particular kind of problem. So when they ask you why you've been away, just say you fell over something at home, hit your head badly, and were taken to the hospital to make sure there wasn't any damage, but now everything's fine. Okay?"

She uttered these last few sentences all in one breath, as if to free herself of a disagreeable and embarrassing task. My mother liked to think of herself as a person who always told the truth, so she was violating one of the fundamental rules of her own identity.

"Okay," I said without comment.

She looked at me again. The conversation wasn't over.

"Antonio . . ."

"Yes?"

"Don't play soccer for a while. Don't tire yourself out, take care of yourself. The doctor said that what happened to you probably won't happen again, but you have to avoid creating conditions that might trigger . . . the problem. We need to be patient, we have the check-up in a few months, and then I'm sure you'll soon be able to go back to doing what you want."

"How long?"

"Right now I don't know exactly . . ."

15

She heaved a sigh. She wasn't used to not knowing how to act. I think my illness gave her an unfamiliar sense of weakness that she found hard to bear.

"We have the check-up in a few months and then we'll know," she went on, making a gesture with her open hand that was meant to be conclusive but expressed only frustration.

Then she repeated the list of rules that had to be followed.

Among other things, the prospect of giving up soccer games after school, followed by drinking lemonade at the stand in the park, struck me as the most humiliating.

It was an unpleasantly simple matter: I had an illness that needed to be kept hidden, and my life wouldn't just change, it would get worse.

"Everything will be fine. There's nothing to worry about," Mom concluded, in a perfect display of cognitive dissonance, just like my father's in the hospital: her words said one thing, her face and her expression said another.

4

As I predicted, things didn't go well.

I was excused from physical education, which didn't make my reintegration any easier. I don't know if my classmates swallowed the story that I'd had a fall at home or if any of them assumed I had a *health problem* that was more serious than the aftereffects of a bruise. I certainly felt as if I was being watched.

It's possible this was the paranoia typical of someone who finds himself in that kind of situation, but I got the feeling that the other kids, the teachers, and even the janitor treated me with deliberate, excessive, hurtful caution. Whenever I passed a small group of my classmates, they all fell suddenly silent, exchanging sympathetic, knowing looks.

I soon started to feel not so much an invalid as a reject. In the morning, urged on by Mom, I'd drag myself to school The rest of the time, I didn't go out. I couldn't play soccer, and I had no desire to give explanations or tell lies to my friends. So I'd spend the afternoons on my own, lounging on the sofa, watching TV without really following any of the programs, bingeing on whatever I found in the fridge or the pantry, and indulging with increasing frequency in gloomy meditations on a world dominated by predestination, illness and death.

I'd become a big reader early, in the third year of elementary school. It was my favorite pastime, unusual for a kid who also played sports. From that point of view, I couldn't have led a more privileged life because our home was full of books of all kinds, including several encyclopedias, and all the works of Salgari, Dumas, and Conan Doyle, as well as a copious collection of Maigrets.

After my seizure and the time in the hospital, I stopped. At most, I'd absently leaf through a few old comics, sprawled on the same sofa where I watched television. I'd lost all desire to read books. If the thought ever crossed my mind, I couldn't figure out how I could have liked them before. It was as if I'd never opened one in my life.

It's hard to say if this apathy was due to the drugs or to my identification with the role of a sick person. Probably both, but what's certain is that the more time passed, the worse the situation got.

My parents couldn't help noticing.

One day in February, my father came to the apartment. He and Mom greeted each other with their usual politeness, which irritated me no end. In particular, I always wondered why Mom, who as far as I knew had been abandoned, didn't harbor or display an honest resentment.

"Next Monday, we're going to Marseilles," Dad said without any preamble. My mother was listening in silence: clearly, she'd already been informed.

"Where?" I said.

"Marseilles, in France."

"What are we going there for?"

He and Mom realized that not everything was working in the therapy I was following. They had their doubts about the amount of drugs I was taking and the oddness of the rules I'd been given. They realized that overall I seemed to be having problems—a brilliant insight, I was about to exclaim, with what was left of my teenage aggressiveness—and that when it came down to it, it was a good idea to get a second opinion and make sure the treatment was the right one or if it needed to be modified in any way.

So they had started making inquiries as to who were the best specialists in *that condition*—I don't think my parents ever uttered the word "epilepsy" in my presence—both in Italy and abroad. This led them to the conclusion that easily the greatest expert on *that condition*, in children and young people, was a Professor Henri Gastaut of Marseilles.

The waiting list to be seen by this luminary was very long, but my father had called his office to ask if there was any way to be seen earlier. It turned out that it was possible to have an appointment in four days because another patient had canceled. Could we come at such short notice? Yes, we could, my father had replied, and had immediately organized the trip—tickets, foreign currency, hotel booking—and now he was here to inform me that all three of us would be leaving for France.

My first impulse was to tell him I didn't want to go to Marseilles; I'd read, or heard on television, that it was a dangerous place. This was just me being contrary. I was annoyed that I'd been presented with a fait accompli; or maybe the thought of going on a trip with my parents, after they'd been separated for years, made me feel unspeakably sad.

But all I did was huff and puff as a mark of protest, and four days later we were in Marseilles.

The city struck me as gray and inhospitable, thanks to the season and the constant rain. The sea was somewhere around, but I don't remember seeing it. Actually, I didn't see anything during those days, except for the hotel, the hospital, and then the hotel again.

The Hôtel de Provence had carpets in the rooms and a vaguely metallic smell, something like cast iron. I don't re-member anything else about the place apart from the fact that my mother had a single room while my father and I shared a double. They behaved toward each other like two acquain-tances, polite and reserved.

It was a sad, awkward situation, and I wished I were grown up, healthy, alone, and a long way away.

5

The Centre Saint-Paul for the treatment of epilepsy was a large, rather anonymous modern building on the outskirts of the city. We took a taxi there, my father on one side, my mother on the other, and me in the middle.

Unlike the hospital where I had been admitted after my seizure, everything at the Saint-Paul worked well, and the atmosphere was one of quiet efficiency. It was like being in another world, even—given how incredibly modern the equipment was—in another time.

We were seen by a young doctor, a colleague of Gastaut's, who handled the preliminary tests. The professor would see me after these, once the records had been completed, he told my parents, who both spoke French fluently. It struck me that I'd never be as natural as that in a language other than Italian.

For two days, they did all kinds of things to me, and I was made to do all kinds of things. My memory of it is confused; the images overlap. Electrodes applied to my head, examination tables, computers, charts, X-rays, and so on; futuristic devices including one that fired colored lights into my eyes in rapid succession, like some kind of psychedelic hallucination.

I remember lots of doctors, lots of nurses, and, above all, lots of children and teenagers in the waiting rooms of the different clinics. Some wore safety helmets; some had teeth missing; some had huge bruises or dressings on their faces and heads.

It was a disturbing sight. I was told their injuries were the result of frequent, violent seizures, typical of some serious types of epilepsy. These kids would lose consciousness, fall disastrously, and break their teeth, or split their heads open.

Looking at them—I saw a great many of them in those three days at the Centre Saint-Paul—I felt two conflicting emotions. On the one hand, it seemed to me that, all things considered, I'd been lucky: things could have been much worse. When it came down to it, I had fainted just once and got off scot-free, no toothless or fearsome grimace to face high school with.

On the other hand, I wondered if I really was safe or if, on the contrary, I didn't run the risk of getting worse and finding myself in the same circle of hell as those clearly unhappy contemporaries of mine.

The moment came to meet Professor Gastaut.

The door of his room opened at eleven o'clock on the dot: the time fixed for the appointment. The first thing I thought when I saw him was that he looked like an actor, like Michel Piccoli, the French movie star known for his confidence and savoir faire.

He conveyed a sense of lively and slightly cocky resolve. He had a thick beard streaked with gray, thick eyebrows, and dark, very mobile eyes, the kind that are always balanced between laughter and anger.

He leafed through my medical records, now and again lingering over one of the papers. At one point, with an expression halfway between amusement and disgust, he muttered something about *fizzy drinks*.

At last, he looked up at me and smiled. "Is there anything you particularly like doing, Antonio? Do you have a talent? Music, drawing, some special skill?" He spoke good Italian and seemed pleased to show it off, even quite smug about it.

The question caught me off guard. "I like drawing," I replied after about ten seconds.

"Would you be able to draw a picture of me? It doesn't need to be more than a sketch."

"Yes . . . I think so."

He handed me a drawing pad and a couple of pencils and, as he had asked, I drew a picture of him, while my mother and my father looked on in considerable surprise.

When I'd finished, I handed him back the sheet of paper, and he looked at it and nodded. I didn't know if he nodded because he liked the drawing or because the fact that I could draw somehow confirmed an intuition or theory of his.

"There are many types of epilepsy," he said finally. "Antonio's isn't serious, and fortunately, the prognosis is good. In a few years, he may not need drugs anymore."

He went on to explain that, in medicine, there are never any absolute certainties, but that, all in all, we could be reasonably optimistic. It wasn't possible to establish the cause of my condition, which made it a classic idiopathic epilepsy, but it was probably due to a trauma during birth. The treatment needed to be redefined and above all simplified. Instead of the four different drugs I'd been taking every day for months, it would be sufficient to take just one. As for the precautions I needed to take, it might be best to avoid boxing, rugby, or wrestling, but otherwise I was free to do what I wanted, even play soccer. He would see me again in three years, and at that time, in all probability, he would be able to discharge me.

We listened to it all, right to the end, increasingly relieved. My mother and father looked like two co-defendants who had just heard the judge read out their acquittal. I, too, obviously, was very pleased. But there was something that Gastaut didn't say but which I wanted to know.

"Why did you make me draw you?" I asked when it was clear that he wanted to hear me ask it.

He smiled, as if playing a little game. "For many years I've been trying to study the possible links between epilepsy and talent, especially artistic talent. I've written a number of articles on the subject. Many great people were epileptics."

"Who were epileptics?" I asked, realizing that this was the first time I'd managed to say the word.

"Just to give a few examples: Aristotle, Pascal, Edgar Allan Poe, Dostoevsky, Handel, Julius Caesar, Flaubert, Maupassant, Berlioz, Newton, Molière, Tolstoy, Leonardo da Vinci, Beethoven, Michelangelo, Socrates, Van Gogh."

I processed this information.

It's strange how the same thing, exactly the same thing, can make us feel so different depending on how we see it, the mental context in which we put it.

Ever since I'd been diagnosed with it, epilepsy had been, as far as I was concerned, a stigma, a sign of inferiority, a disgraceful blemish that had to be hidden. After Gastaut's words, after hearing that list of geniuses who had all apparently had a problem similar to mine, my inner world now turned a hundred and eighty degrees, as if moving from darkness to light. I had felt like a reject, and, all at once, for the very same material reason, I felt almost one of the chosen, a member of a special category of superior beings.

"Please sign your drawing," Gastaut said, in an almost formal tone. I signed it, and it seemed natural to me, as if I were signing a contract with my new life, which was starting at that moment.

He stood up, shook hands with us, repeated that he would see us again in three years and walked us to the door.

"Oh, Antonio?" he said with his hand on the handle.

"Yes?"

"You can go back to them."

"What?"

"Fizzy drinks."

6

With that unaggressive treatment and the sense of normality that Gastaut's diagnosis had restored to me, life resumed at an ordinary pace.

The creeping depression into which I had sunk after my stay in the hospital vanished overnight. I went back to doing what I'd done before, including playing soccer and having soda. In other words, I again blended in with my contemporaries, while at the same time wanting to be very different from them. All teenagers suffer from the same schizophrenia. They do all they can to be the same and dream of being different.

I also started reading again.

The three years passed slowly, almost statically: a kind of eternal present, an elusive season filled with daydreams rather than significant events.

The fact is, instead of having experiences, I imagined them. In the magical future of my dreams, I wrote books, drew comics, made animated films with characters who became as famous, popular, and beloved as Disney or Marvel characters.

I imagined an existence as vague as it was wonderful, made up of trips around the world, adventures, romantic encounters with beautiful and seductive girls.

Life in the real world was a little more boring. I'd like to be able to say that my adolescence was full of unforgettable episodes, but unfortunately, it wasn't.

My most exciting memories of that period are dreams I had and the times when I had them: during a walk, lying on the bed listening to music, sitting on the steps in the playground during a sit-in the first year of high school.

Things that actually *happened*, though, were few and far between.

I had a brief fling with a girl my age named Mara. We didn't talk in those days about "being in a relationship"—not that the words would have been the right ones to describe our rapid encounter and even more rapid separation.

We met at a party; we went to the cinema together a couple of times, we walked around holding hands for a few weeks, we exchanged a few kisses and a few very awkward caresses in damp doorways. They were my very first sexual experiences—if I may put it so bluntly—and that's the only reason they haven't been consigned to oblivion. The whole thing ended within a few months, without either of us losing our virginity and without the subject even coming up.

Apart from this interlude with Mara, clumsy but real, I mostly devoted myself, in accordance with my character, to imaginary loves. In particular, I fell in love at a distance with a girl who looked like Sophie Marceau, and who never even noticed me, being too busy going out with twenty-five-year-olds equipped with flashy convertibles and high-powered motorbikes. This, with hindsight, was a stroke of luck: if she'd noticed me and we'd actually spoken, I'd have ended up giving her the poems I had written for her and subjecting myself forever to ridicule.

Another thing I remember—it seems like one of those distressing dreams you have just before waking, but it was frighteningly real—is the suicide of a boy in my school, a boy the same age as me, whom I knew only by sight.

A girl in my class told me what had happened, on the way home after school. She told me while we were passing a dry cleaner's, from which came that unmistakable smell of steam, irons, and starch. Ever since then, the smell of a dry cleaner's has reminded me of that slightly clumsy-looking boy, his forehead and nose covered in acne, who at about eight that morning, instead of coming to school, had climbed over the railing on the roof of his building, and let himself fall. Seven floors of a modern apartment block is twenty-one meters, that was the first thing I thought, and I asked myself if, as you dropped more than twenty meters, you had time to realize what you'd done and think you might have done something different.

Yes, I immediately answered my own question. Once, on a bet, I'd thrown myself from the ten-meter Olympic diving board, and I'd certainly had time to think. So would he, that was for sure: and this struck me as the most terrible part of the whole business.

I searched my memory for clues, symptoms, warning signs pointing to what had happened. We all searched for them, I imagine, to convince ourselves that he was different, and that what had happened to him couldn't happen to us.

But I didn't find any symptoms, any warning signs. The truth is that Enrico—that was his name, though I don't think I ever uttered it—appeared normal, just like everyone else. There was a lot of speculation, but nobody would ever really understand what had driven him to it.

If he'd had some deep-rooted issue—something that predisposed him to do what he did—it was so well hidden that nobody had managed to see it, which was why nobody could remember it.

Enrico's death was the first senseless act I'd experienced in my life. The first revelation of chaos. Something so absurd and enormous as to confuse the mind that tried to make head or tail of it.

Maybe it was to take shelter from that dizzying sense of absurdity, to protect ourselves from the abyss, that after two days, as if by tacit agreement, we stopped talking about him.

We forgot him, as if he had never existed.

He *had* never existed.

At elementary school I was in a small group at the top of the class. I was good at everything, and very good at drawing and mathematics. The teacher would say that it was obvious I was my father's son, my father being a mathematician. I liked hearing this as a child, but as I grew, it began to annoy me until it became almost unbearable.

When I started in middle school, I settled, for various reasons, into a comfortable mediocrity. I didn't study much, contented myself with getting pass marks. Belonging to the club at the top of the class became a distant childhood memory.

One day, I met my elementary teacher. We hadn't seen each other in a long time, and she asked me how I was doing at school, if I was still as good at mathematics. I replied that I didn't give a damn about mathematics, that I hated numbers and formulas, that when I grew up, I would do a job that had nothing to do with all that stuff. I remember her sad, surprised look. And I well remember the feeling of dejection, of guilt, almost of shame, that overcame me for what I had said to her, and the way I had said it; for the indistinct lump of weakness and resentment I sensed behind my words.

Precisely because those three years were long, precisely because I'd quickly forgotten about myself, it struck me as almost absurd when one day, my father told me he had made another appointment with Professor Gastaut. It was May, and the visit had been fixed for June, immediately after the end of classes.

"Why do we have to go in June?" I replied angrily.

He looked at me for a moment or two, bewildered. He couldn't figure out the tone of my voice or, especially, the meaning of my question, which must indeed, in its reference to June, have seemed incomprehensible. The fact was, with those two innocuous pills a day—the same drug, morning and evening—I had found a balance.

I was living normally; the medication didn't bother me at

all, there were no side effects; taking it was like cleaning my teeth, in other words, something you do more than once a day without even noticing. Why run the risk of upsetting that balance?

I had forgotten—dismissed—the word epilepsy; I had forgotten the fact that I was an epileptic, even the stigma of disability and exclusion that had been with me always in the months between my stay in the hospital and my consultation with Gastaut was long gone. I didn't want to go back to it. I didn't want to be afraid.

"What do you mean?" he asked, lighting a cigarette, still looking puzzled. "When do you think we should go?"

The question was a simple, unexceptionable one, and that was why I got even more annoyed.

"I'll only just have finished school, and already I have to do that? In June? Maybe I'd like to go to the seaside and relax, rather than having to go to Marseilles. Can't we wait a few months, maybe till the autumn or the winter? What a drag!"

My father made an exasperated face. Having to deal with his only child had become increasingly difficult over the years. He took a deep breath and spoke deliberately slowly.

"Listen to me, Antonio. When he saw you, Gastaut said he would see you again after three years. The three years are up: it was February, remember? Apart from anything else, I found out that he's retiring soon and will only do private consultations, outside the center, without all that equipment. We can get it all over with in two days. Then you can enjoy your vacation."

"I'm fine. What's the point?"

"Yes, you're fine, thank heavens, but you're on medication. You're not planning to take it all your life, are you? It's a barbiturate, a psychoactive drug, and, well, it isn't a good idea to take psychoactive drugs if you don't need to."

Obviously, he was right. I looked for some argument that wasn't ridiculous, but couldn't find one. So I walked boorishly away without saying goodbye.

Two weeks later, we left for Marseilles.

7

My mother didn't come with us. She had an international conference in Florence where she was due to give a paper. She'd told me that if I wanted, she wouldn't go but I'd replied in an adult tone that she shouldn't even think about it, the conference mattered a lot to her, and she shouldn't give it up.

That, at least, was a relief: just the thought of repeating the trip we'd made three years earlier, with both my parents, had made me feel as if I was suffocating.

We got to Marseilles in the evening. We already had my complete medical records with us because, over the past few days, I'd had tests and EEGs. Gastaut would see me the following morning, and later that afternoon, we'd fly home.

The hotel was in an unremarkable modern building, definitely more comfortable than the one we'd been in the first time. It was close to the Canebière, the most famous street in Marseilles, which links the middle-class neighborhood of Réformés to the Vieux Port.

After settling in, exchanging only the few words required, we went out to look for somewhere to eat.

The area where our hotel was looked like a normal French

city, a normal European city, in other words, a place like our hometown, where we could feel relatively at ease.

We soon realized that this impression was partial at best. As we proceeded toward the harbor, in fact, Marseilles turned, before our eyes, into a kind of urban metropolis; every corner presided over by prostitutes and pimps, its streets crisscrossed by groups of hungry-looking youths and punctuated with convenience stores filled to the brim like miniature bazaars, boarded-up shop fronts, restaurants smelling of spices and fried food, dubious-looking cafés and porn cinemas. On two or three occasions, we were obliged to avoid or step over men lying slumped on the ground: drunks, junkies, or just hopeless down-and-outs.

My father and I didn't speak, but we could sense each other's growing unease. It was dark by now, and overall the streets conveyed a sense of the unknown, a sense of danger. I'd have liked to say that it might be better to turn back, but I couldn't somehow do it, I couldn't find the words: my father might take offense, might think that I considered him incapable of handling an emergency.

I think he too was thinking something similar, and that he would have preferred to return to less inhospitable territory, but like me he said nothing. He lit a cigarette and looked around, trying not to make it too obvious that he was looking around. As if somebody might be bothered by his excessive curiosity and call us out on it.

At a certain point, we heard yells behind us. We turned just in time to see a short, thin boy running on the other side of the street. Behind him were two policemen. One of them, in particular, had the powerful, threatening stride of a rugby player running after an opponent. Whenever a passerby got in his way, he shoved them aside without even slowing down. The boy was quick, but the policeman must have been a trained athlete and gradually lessened the distance between them.

The scene had its own wild, rhythmic beauty.

The last phase of the pursuit took place in parallel with the tram lines, which seemed almost like an athletics track, intended specifically for this pitiless sport. In the end, the policeman caught up with the fugitive, grabbed him and flung him to the ground. They were about fifty meters from us, and I went closer, curious to see what was going to happen. I had the distinct impression that my father had been on the point of saying something—where are you going? let it be—but at the last moment had held back.

By now, the policeman, who had fair hair and looked more German than French, had lifted the black boy bodily from the ground, shoved him up against a metal shutter, and was searching him. Almost immediately, he found something on him, something I couldn't make out, but that made him angry. He put the object in his pocket, yelled something incomprehensible, and started beating the boy with a violence I'd never seen before. By the time the other policeman arrived, a small group of people had formed, all with dark skin and eyes filled with fear and hate.

The two policemen talked frantically among themselves. The first one handcuffed the suspect behind his back, while the other, who was bald and bony, yelled something at the group of hostile onlookers—there were about fifteen of them now, maybe more.

"What did he say?" I asked my father.

"To move back, or someone was going to get killed."

But they didn't move back, except by a few centimeters, and their expressions were becoming increasingly aggressive. Some shouted, some spat in the direction of the policemen, who were now looking decidedly worried. The bald one took out his pistol and aimed it at the little crowd. There was a hint of hysteria in his angry voice. This time there was a ripple of reaction, but nobody ran away.

We were ten or so meters away. My father touched me on the shoulder and said, "Let's get out of here."

"Wait," I said, not moving. He didn't insist.

The policeman aimed his gun in the air and fired twice; a few moments later, almost as if responding to a call, sirens wailed, getting closer. The crowd scattered like a flock of birds.

Two cars pulled up, and more men in uniform got out; the flashing lights kept working, intermittently illuminating the scene like special effects in a disco.

The boy was bundled into one of the cars, which left in a pointless screeching of tires.

We had a passable dinner in a nasty restaurant near the hotel. I'd have liked to talk about what had happened, what we had seen, but I realized I didn't have the words, didn't know how to speak to my father.

This gave me an unexpected stab of regret. It also confused me. It was as if the consistency I clung to, the whole foundation of my rebelliousness toward my family, had been damaged by that involuntary impulse.

We went to bed, and I lay there for a long time with my eyes wide open. I thought again about what had happened and listened to my father sleeping in the next bed. His breathing was like the rustle of trampled leaves. Now and again, he would mutter a few meaningless words.

I thought, with an unpleasant sense of foreboding, about the consultation that awaited me.

I fell asleep immediately after telling myself I was bound to stay awake, and did something not very original: I went from thinking about Gastaut to *dreaming* about Gastaut.

He was serious, much less cordial and friendly than the first time. He was sitting with my mother on a sofa in a room, unlike the office in which he had seen me three years earlier, a room I had never seen before. After looking through the papers he told me that, unfortunately, things hadn't gone as he had hoped and that, unfortunately, my *epilepsy* wasn't so slight after all. I would have to go back to the old treatment and stop drinking fizzy drinks and playing soccer. It was important to realize that I would never have a normal life. At this point, my mother cut in and said she'd told me I shouldn't play soccer.

Then I noticed that my father was also there in the dream.

But he was off to one side, not saying anything, and I felt a strange, inexplicable tenderness toward him.

8

We were due to present ourselves at the reception desk of the Centre Saint-Paul at ten.

We had breakfast, my father paid for the room, and we took a taxi to the center, carrying with us our two old, small, half-empty leather suitcases. It was 1983, and trolley suitcases hadn't yet been invented, although these days, we think they've always been around.

The idea was to go straight to the airport from the center immediately after the consultation. Maybe there was a touch of superstition in such a tight schedule, or maybe it was just the fact that the next day my father had exams at the university and had arranged things so that he wouldn't have to postpone them.

It was almost summer, the air was clear; there was a pleasant breeze, and it wasn't too hot or too cool.

The city looked bright and friendly; it made you feel like visiting it.

The center was different from the way I remembered it. The people were different. The thing that most struck me was the absence of children and young people with helmets or broken teeth. Was it a coincidence? Or were they now summoned on particular days or seen in separate rooms so as not to upset the less severely affected patients? Or had advances in treatment eliminated some of the more unpleasant consequences of seizures?

I was directed to the final tests, which required equipment that existed only at the Centre Saint-Paul. Immediately after them, I would see the professor.

It's strange. I remember very clearly all the tests I underwent the first time at the Centre Saint-Paul, even though those happened further back in time. And yet I don't remember what they did to me that morning. I mean, I don't remember a single thing.

It's as if after showing up at reception, I had been drugged, and the effects of the drug had worn off only when we were admitted to the waiting room outside Gastaut's office.

That's the point at which my memory picks up the thread.

We still had to wait, the nurse told us. There had been an emergency that had forced them to delay that morning's appointments, but we would be seen shortly.

After exchanging a few banal words, asking each other if there might be a risk of missing our plane and telling each other there wasn't, given that it was still several hours until the flight, we simultaneously took out our books. My father had with him Goffredo Parise's *Sillabari*; I had J. D. Salinger's *Franny and Zooey*, which I much preferred to *The Catcher in the Rye* and was reading for the second time.

About ten minutes went by, then Gastaut opened the door, and asked us to come in.

He greeted me, shaking my hand and calling me by my first name, then greeted my father, shaking his hand and calling him professor. So he remembered us, which impressed me.

"You're all grown up now, Antonio. Do you still draw?" he asked in his excellent, if strongly French-accented Italian. I gave a slight smile, and he concentrated on the test results.

His examination of my medical record lasted a few minutes, while I couldn't help thinking about my nightmares and the possibility that they had been a premonition.

My father scrutinized Gastaut's face in search of clues as to the verdict he was about to deliver. The only sound in the room was the hum of distant equipment.

At last, Gastaut put the file down on the desk, closed it, and looked at us: first one, then the other. If he was trying to create suspense, he was succeeding.

"Everything is as we expected."

I breathed. I exchanged glances with my father, who reached out a hand and squeezed my leg just above the knee. It was a gesture that should have bothered me, I thought. Instead, it didn't bother me at all.

"Antonio appears cured," Gastaut resumed. "The tests are good, but there's still one test to do, to be on the safe side."

"What test?" my father asked.

He explained it to us. To be certain that I was completely cured and could, therefore, stop taking the drugs, it was necessary to check how my brain reacted in conditions of stress.

In practice, he told us, I would have to go without sleep for two nights in a row, every eight hours taking some pills that he would give me and that would help me to stay awake. At the same time, I was to stay off the drug I'd been taking every day, twice a day for the last three years.

If even with sleep deprivation, the elimination of the drug, and the administration of those pills—amphetamines, probably, but neither my father nor I asked what they were—nothing happened, it meant I was fine and could devote myself to the normal life of an eighteen-year-old boy, forgetting all about hospitals, EEGs, barbiturates, and, above all, neurologists.

Technically, this procedure was called a provocative test. These days it's forbidden by medical ethics, I've been told by a psychiatrist friend, but at the time, it was still used.

"And when should he do this test?" my father asked, somewhat dismayed.

Gastaut looked at him as you might look at someone who's asked a rather strange question. "Immediately. Don't sleep tonight, don't sleep tomorrow night, and come back here the morning after next. If everything's fine, we'll say goodbye forever."

"But we're supposed to be going home today. Our flight's booked . . ."

"My dear professor, if you'd rather, we can put this final test off until a later date. We'll have to make another appointment, and that won't be before the end of the year. In the meantime, Antonio will have to continue with the barbiturate for several more months. In my opinion, it would be better to do it immediately, but, of course, the decision is yours." There was a slight, ever so polite hint of irritation in Gastaut's voice.

"Could he have a seizure?"

"I don't think so, but yes, in theory, it could happen. It's . . . how can I put this? Yes, it's unlikely, but not impossible."

"What do we do if that happens?"

"Come straight here, even at night, and we'll do what has to be done. If he does have a seizure, it means he isn't cured, and will have to keep taking his medication. Unlikely, I repeat, but not impossible."

My father let maybe half a minute go by, then turned to me. "Are you up for it?" I nodded, not so much because I was sure I felt up for it, but because of the way he'd asked me. Man to man, showing me respect.

"All right, we'll make arrangements," he concluded, getting to his feet.

Gastaut said it was the right decision, told us again that a seizure was unlikely, gave my father a box of the pills I would have to take every eight hours, and concluded by saying that he would see us in two days, at nine on the dot.

"Do whatever you like during these two days. Do physical exercise; drink coffee and wine, if you like—without overdoing it, obviously. Think of it as a holiday. I'll see you the day after tomorrow."

9

"What now?" I asked as we waited outside the hospital for the taxi which the ultra-efficient reception staff had called for us. We'd already spoken to Mom, as we had previously arranged to call her. She had been a little worried, but my father had done a good job of reassuring her, telling her only the most essential elements of the truth.

"Let's go back to the hotel," Dad said, "and let's hope they have a room available for two nights. Otherwise we'll have to look for another hotel. Then we have to find a travel agency to reschedule our flight. Then . . . then we'll see," he concluded, loosening his tie and lighting a cigarette.

Our room had already been taken, but there was another one available, a larger, more expensive one, with a nice view. My father shrugged and said we'd take it for two nights.

"Although I think, at night, it's best not to stay here at all, or there's a risk we'll fall asleep," he said, turning to me, while the receptionist dealt with the new registration.

"But you can sleep," I replied.

He looked at me, seemed about to reply, then merely shook his head.

"Am I talking bullshit?" I asked.

The corner of his mouth turned up. "Yes. But given the situation, it doesn't seem like much of a sin. Talking bullshit, I mean."

My father didn't usually use swear words. He was very careful, certainly more than my mother, and I had rarely, and then only in exceptional circumstances, heard him say words like "bullshit." Never, anyway, in the casual way he'd used it just then. Something was happening that I couldn't quite grasp.

We settled into the new room and immediately realized that, among other things, we had to look for a clothes shop or a department store. We had no clean shirts or underwear, having packed only enough for one day and one night.

We went out, got two completely bland cheese sandwiches and two beers, had them on a bench, and then went to the travel agency we'd been directed to in the hotel.

Changing the tickets took longer than expected. The clerk didn't seem like the brightest spark: even though my father spoke almost perfect French, he kept asking him to repeat, indicating that he didn't understand. He was assuming the irritable expression of someone who has much more important things to do than deal with boring trivia involving a boring Italian customer.

I got annoyed and wished I knew the language so that I could take part in the conversation and tell the guy that he was a dickhead, or something like that. I was surprised to discover that I'd have liked to support my father, because I felt the man was showing him a lack of respect.

He, though, was calm and looked strangely youthful. In the hotel, he had taken off his jacket and tie, because it was hot; his hair was uncombed, which almost never happened, and it seemed as if the obnoxious clerk was actually putting him in a good mood.

In the end, we got our tickets, and my father said good-bye with excessive cordiality, which strongly suggested he was taking the piss out of the guy.

Out in the street, we looked each other in the eyes, and I had the feeling that this was the first time we'd ever done that.

"Now, let's look for a phone," he said. "I have to call the faculty and tell them I won't be there tomorrow."

"Next year I'm enrolling at university," I said, after ten seconds or so.

"I know. Do you have any ideas yet?"

"No. Had you already decided, before your last year at high school?"

He made a vague gesture. "I'd known I was going to study mathematics, or maybe physics, since middle school. I never considered any alternatives."

He lit a cigarette. I wondered how many he smoked a day. Too many, anyway. We walked in silence, searching for a phone booth.

"What about Mom?" I asked after turning the question around in my head for two or three minutes, unsure whether or not to ask it.

49

"What about her?"

"Did she know which major to enroll in?"

"I think so. She'd always thought about studying literature, something on the arts side anyway. The choice of art history came during university. She never thought of studying engineering or medicine, for example."

"Some of my friends have known what they're going to do at university since middle school. I always thought that was strange."

"It depends," he said, stubbing out the end of his cigarette against a wall and throwing it into a trash can.

"The children of doctors want to study medicine; the children of lawyers want to study law. But how do you know at the age of twelve if you have a talent for a particular subject, or if you'll even like it? In my opinion, they just want to imitate their parents, or rather, their fathers, because these are the kinds of students whose mothers don't work."

"Yes, it's often not a good idea. My schoolmates, who inherited their father's line of work, never seemed very happy."

"I was only ever once in your office at the university."

"I remember. You were six or seven. You felt bad that my room was so small."

He was right; I'd felt really bad. I knew my father was friends with great scientists from all over the world; therefore, he must have been important; therefore, his office should have been fitting to his importance. Before seeing it, I'd imagined it as a kind of drawing room with big, bright windows, complete with scientific equipment, and lots of books. The one accurate element of my fantasy had proved to be the books.

It was a fairly small room, with a single, normal-sized window, and it was indeed full of books, which were everywhere: on the shelves, on the desk, and even in unsteady piles shoved up against the walls.

It was a disappointment, but I would never have admitted it, nor would I ever have thought that my father had noticed, let alone that he would remember it after so many years.

I couldn't think of anything else to say: the normality of this conversation was quite disconcerting. I shoved my hands in my pockets and continued walking in silence beside my father until we found a public telephone.

He made a couple of calls before he found the person he was looking for: some university assistant or employee. What I found hard to understand was how formal Dad was with everybody. He was different from Mom, even in this. She quickly and easily got on first-name terms with whoever she was talking to: in many ways, she belonged to a different, later period than the one in which she had been born and raised.

"It's fine, now we're on holiday," my father said when he had finished. "Sometimes you think you're indispensable, that without you the world would collapse, or at least that it wouldn't be able to keep going. Then something like this happens, and you realize: a) that you're not indispensable; and b) that it's not such a bad thing, not being indispensable."

"So, what do we do?"

"Underwear. We need underwear, that's essential. Shirts too. Let's look for a department store and spend a few francs."

We asked directions of a thin woman with a pronounced chin, smiley and rather excitable, who, after exchanging a few words, asked us, in Italian, if we were Italian. She was Italian, too, had moved to Marseilles with her parents just before the war and had been living there for forty-five years, although the city wasn't the same anymore, it had become a dangerous place—not that she was a racist, she wanted to make that clear—but with all these young Algerians and Moroccans and Tunisians, Marseilles didn't seem like a French city anymore, and maybe the best thing would be to leave, but there were also lots of Italians in Marseilles, and besides, Italians and Marseilles people are similar in some ways because both of them speak as if they were singing, and why were we here, if that wasn't an indiscreet question, because Marseilles wasn't a city for tourists, it was beautiful, heaven knows, but a bit dangerous if you didn't know how to get around, which was why she didn't think we were tourists, and she was sorry, she knew she was a chatterbox but she was so happy to have the chance to speak Italian she thought she'd never stop.

My father stemmed her flow politely and effectively with a few well-placed lies. He told her we were making Marseilles our base for visiting Provence; that we had lost a suitcase and needed to buy a few items of clothing and some other things, so we were looking for a department store. Could she point us in the direction of one, please?

She pointed one out to us, advised us to be careful in some

areas of the city, not to go near the Vieux Port or the Panier in the evening, or even in the morning really, then she wished us a happy holiday in Provence: in a few days the lavender would be in bloom, which was a wonderful sight, but maybe that was why we'd come at this time of year. She concluded by saying that it was really nice that a handsome young man like me should go on holiday with his father, when there must have been lots of girls who'd have liked to be with me.

I avoided telling the woman that, as far as I was aware, things weren't quite like that, and that if there were lots of girls who wanted to be with me, they must have been very discreet about it, because I had never noticed.

In the end, we managed to get away, thanked Signora Marta Monicelli—she had even found the opportunity to tell us her name, making it clear that, as far as she knew, she wasn't related to the film director—said goodbye to her and headed for the store.

It was a nice, modern place, the kind that used to cheer me up back then because you could find everything in it. We hurried to the clothing department, and stocked up on white and blue shirts, socks and underwear. We wouldn't need trousers, but Dad insisted that we buy new jeans.

From clothing, we went on to visit the other departments: fancy goods, electronics, books—we bought a tourist guide to Marseilles and its surroundings—and finally food. More than anything else, I remember the cheese counter, with those smells halfway between scent and stink, which even now, as I write, make my mouth water. The names on the lined-up price tags sounded like a children's nursery rhyme or the members of a soccer team: Comté, Reblochon, Camembert, Brie, Roquefort, Chèvre, Beaufort, Saint-Nectaire, Cantal, Cancoillotte, Brocciu.

"I'm starting to feel hungry."

"Me too," Dad replied. "These must be better than the yellow stuff that was in our sandwiches."

"What shall we do?"

"Instinctively, I'd buy three or four, with a bit of bread and a nice bottle of red wine, and go and eat in a park somewhere."

"But?"

"But we have a lot of time to kill, and we have to stay awake. If we skip dinner like that, the night'll feel really long. Better to adopt a different strategy."

I wondered if my father had ever talked this way before, because I sensed a change. Not only in his vocabulary—"instinctively" and "strategy" were terms I didn't think I'd ever heard him use—but also in the rhythm and even the intonation.

Maybe it was just that I'd started to notice what he was saying and the way he said it, which was why I felt that I was discovering something when in fact, it had always been there.

"What now?"

He looked at his watch. "It's almost seven. Let's go to the hotel, take a shower, read, have a look at the guide. Then, let's put on our new shirts and go out to look for a restaurant that's better than the one last night. What do you think?"

I said I thought that was a good idea and made to set off.

"Antonio . . ."

"Yes?"

"Here," he said, handing me the blister with the pills that Gastaut had given him. The ones to stay awake, although I didn't know what they were. "Maybe you can take the first one now. Then one every eight hours, he said. Anyway, you keep hold of them."

IO

We were lying on our beds, in T-shirts and underpants. My father was studying the Marseilles guidebook, and I was reading Salinger.

I'd also brought *The Name of the Rose* with me. It had been out for three years, everyone had read it, everyone *liked* it, which was why, to live up to my image as a nonconformist young intellectual, I'd kept my distance from it, slavishly imitating, as it happens, my mother's attitude.

But when the fuss had died down, even she had bought the book in paperback, read it, and actually liked it, whereas as a rule, I would have expected a condescending put-down. That had given me the green light, and just as we were about to leave, I'd thrown it into my suitcase.

I hadn't started it yet, though, because I couldn't tear myself away from *Franny and Zooey*. I was both proud and embarrassed to recognize myself in the self-importance of the characters. They were simultaneously immature and profound, which I thought was great.

I saw in them what seemed to be my own way of thinking, and there were some passages where I had the impression I was actually looking at myself. My faults—or what I liked to think were my faults—were there, but depicted in such a way that I could feel proud of them. I would underline and copy out extracts and pieces of dialogue, and in copying them, I made them mine.

"What a strange feeling," Dad said suddenly, looking up from the Marseilles guidebook.

"What is?"

"I can't remember how long it's been since I had two whole days in front of me with no commitments, no obligations, nothing particular to do. That's what's strange."

I turned to him. "You know, when I look at you grown-ups, I think you're trapped by things you don't actually care about. How does that happen? *When* does it happen?"

He pulled himself up into a sitting position, with his back propped against the headboard. He closed the guidebook after folding down a corner of the page he'd been reading to mark the place.

"It's impossible to establish when. It isn't the result of a sudden change, it happens one day after the other, like a slow landslide that you're hardly aware of. You don't realize it until years later. You burden yourself with superfluous things—objects, commitments, personal relationships—and all these things become just so many invisible threads that weave their way around you, a bit more every day, like a spider's web."

I also sat up, in a movement identical to his earlier one. I put my book down on the bed, still open, with the white cover faceup. "If you're aware of it, why don't you do anything to free yourself?"

"Well, that's the trap. You know you're wasting a lot of your time on pointless things, and yet, you can't get out of them. Do you know Cavafy?"

"Who's that?"

"A Greek poet, though he spent most of his life in Alexandria, in Egypt. One of his poems is on that very theme. It's called: 'As Best You Can.'" He paused, as if wondering whether to go on or change the subject. Then he said, "Would you like to hear it?"

"Yes," I replied, feeling slightly uncomfortable.

He touched his chin, as if to focus his mind and remember, but it was clear that he, too, felt uncomfortable reciting a poem to his son who was nearly eighteen, but whom he barely knew. We were entering uncharted territory.

He cleared his throat.

> *And if you cannot shape your life as you want,*
> *at least try this,*
> *as best you can: do not debase it*
> *by too much contact with the world,*
> *by too much activity and talk.*
> *Do not debase it by taking it around,*
> *dragging it with you, exposing it*
> *to the daily madness*
> *of encounters and invitations,*
> *until it becomes a bothersome stranger.*

The lines lingered in the air for a long time.

"It's beautiful," I said at last. "Do you mind repeating it?

I'd like to write it in my notebook." Speaking to my father like that, in that polite, circumspect way, I wondered what was happening.

He recited it again, slowly, and I transcribed it carefully, on a right-hand page of my almost new notebook.

These days, Cavafy has become fashionable; his words often worn with overuse. But back then, they sounded in all their force, intact and resplendent. They're still there, in that old notebook, dated the beginning of June 1983.

The border between before and after.

"Anyway," Dad said, "there are a lot of things to see in Marseilles. It may not be a city for tourists, as our friend Marta said, but we won't be bored tomorrow."

"Right now, though, let's go and eat."

"Yes, you're right," he said, getting nimbly off the bed.

11

The hotel doorman recommended a restaurant facing the Vieux Port. The owner was his cousin, he said. He would call him to book a table for us and advise him to treat us well. That way, we'd be able to try real, traditional Marseilles cuisine: we particularly shouldn't miss panisses fris, tapenade on toast, and, of course, bouillabaisse.

To get to Chez Papa—that was the name of the restaurant— we, again, walked along the Canebière.

It was the same as the previous evening, but it didn't look so hostile now and the faces of the people that populated it seemed less threatening. Maybe this was due to the fact that it wasn't dark yet, and that we had a specific goal, with directions on how to get there, so we didn't feel lost and vaguely in danger.

The place where we'd witnessed the arrest was quiet. I glanced at the ground, between the tram tracks, almost as if hoping to find traces of what had happened, maybe some spatters of blood from the beating, but there was nothing.

As we walked, I was thinking of the fact that, in all probability, I had never really *talked* to my father. I mean: of course we'd talked, but always—apart from times in my childhood before my parents separated, of which I had no memory—I had been aware of an obstacle between us, a detachment, a grudging tolerance. All I got from him were clumsy attempts to live up to the stereotype of a father figure.

Whenever we met, he would make an effort to be natural and spontaneous. Obviously. he didn't succeed, because it's impossible to be spontaneous to order. "Be spontaneous" is the most paradoxical and impracticable of injunctions, whether coming from other people, or ourselves.

On the other hand, if anyone had asked him about his relationship with his only child, my father would certainly have spoken of a silent hostility that had grown with time, that he couldn't understand and toward which he didn't know how to behave.

That had been the state of play for some years now, but I became aware of it only during our walk along the Canebière, toward Chez Papa.

When we got to the restaurant, we were greeted by Monsieur Dominic, our doorman's cousin, forewarned of our arrival. He showed us to a table with a white-and-red-check tablecloth and a view of the boats in the Vieux Port. There were boats as far as the eye could see, moored at dozens of wooden jetties arranged at right angles to the two large principal quays. Many of these boats had sails, and the overall effect was of an endless expanse of trees and ropes through which the setting sun filtered in a thousand rays. It was twenty past nine when it disappeared completely below the distant horizon.

Ordering was simplicity itself. We asked for what we had been recommended, along with a carafe of Provençal cask rosé.

When the starters arrived, Dad filled my glass—for a moment I thought he was going to pour me just a finger and dilute it with water, as he used to do when I was small— then filled his and raised it toward me, making it gleam in the light. We toasted and drank: the wine was good, cold, and deceptively light.

Noticing how I was enjoying the bouillabaisse, he recalled that as a boy, I'd never wanted to eat fish because I was afraid of the bones; all I would eat were fish fingers. That made another two, or rather three, unexpected details that contrasted with the idea I had of my father. I mean: that he had noticed that I didn't want to eat fish, that I liked fish fingers, and that he remembered.

We finished all the food, emptied the carafe of rosé, told Monsieur Dominic that we had eaten very well—it was true—and asked for the bill.

He brought it to us together with a little plate of biscuits and two small glasses of brandy on the house. The tables were now all occupied, and there was a calm but lively atmosphere, something from another time, as if we were in the 1960s or even earlier.

My father looked around, smiling like a little boy.

Until that moment, if I'd been asked to describe his face, I'd have found it hard to do so. Of course, I would have mentioned his slightly prominent nose, his glasses, his dark eyes, his thick hair streaked with gray. But I wouldn't have been able to say—because I'd never noticed—that he had a dimple in his chin, long eyelashes, and a scar over his left eyebrow. How was it possible that I'd never paid any attention to it?

"What's that scar?" I asked.

"What scar?" he replied. Then he saw in which direction I was pointing. He touched it, as if to check that it was still there. He drank a little brandy and lit a cigarette.

"It happened because of your mother."

"So she did hit you at least once."

My father laughed. A quick, genuine laugh, before replying:

"No, no. Though I did get it because of her, in a way."

The laughter faded and gave way to a vaguely pensive expression.

"I haven't thought about it in ages."

"What happened?"

"Do you know about student fraternities?"

"Yes, from our PE teacher in middle school. He'd studied medicine but never graduated, and in his stories, his university years were a golden age. He'd been somebody in his fraternity. Then his friends had graduated and become doctors, and he'd ended up teaching physical education."

"You know something?"

"What?"

"Sometimes, when I talk to you, in my mind, I still see you when you were a little boy, and I'm surprised to hear you express yourself like that. In such a polished, adult way, I mean."

I didn't know what to say in reply, so I simply nodded,

which always works because the meaning is put into it by the person you're talking to. I let about twenty seconds go by before answering.

"So? What's the story with the scar?"

He smiled, looking into the distance. "When it happened, your mother was a freshman while I was in my fourth year. According to student terminology, I was a four-stamp."

"What does that mean?"

"That there were four rubber stamps in my university record book, one for each academic year. There were even some people who had ten. People who hadn't finished their courses, but still hung around, eternal students. Many of them, like your PE teacher, would never graduate. And, you're right, it would be the best days of their lives. The most amusing time for them was the beginning of the academic year."

"Why?"

"Because at that time the seniors, especially these eternal students, would go in search of freshers and play stupid pranks on them: get them to buy drinks, sometimes just get them to pay up. From a legal point of view, I think they committed various offenses, and extortion was certainly one of them. Anyway, the way it worked was, the most determined frat boys would hang around the university in groups of four or five. They'd identify the freshers and surround them. One by one, I mean. The length of the pranks and their level of stupidity—and sometimes they were very stupid—depended on who the frat boys were and how the freshers reacted."

"Didn't anyone rebel?"

"Not usually. It's like what happens in barracks, between veterans and new recruits. The newcomers are scared and alone; they don't know the background, the environment they're in. They don't know what might happen. In general, the freshmen played along with it, because most of the time, it was just a game. They'd agree to have their legs pulled, even to be knocked about a bit, they'd pay up, and that was that."

"How many times could something like that happen to you?"

"Just once, there was a specific rule. At the end of the ritual, you were issued a card—they called it the parchment—that showed you'd paid—a kind of safe passage. If you were stopped by another group of seniors, you'd show it, and they were obliged to let you go. So basically, in most cases, it was quite harmless, and after a few days, it was all over. Then the frat boys would go on to other things. Parties, drunken binges, group visits to brothels, which were still open then, and legal."

There was something slightly different in the inflection of his voice as he said these last words, about brothels being still open and legal.

"But sometimes things didn't go so well. Maybe the fresher didn't want to put up with these little injustices—which sometimes weren't so little. Or else the seniors were more stupid or nastier, and they overdid it. If the two things coincided, it might turn quite unpleasant. The stupidest prank was when they took the fresher, especially if he didn't play along with them, and threw him in the fountain. Remember, it was November and quite cold."

"But did they do this to girls too?"

"A lot depended on who the frat boys were. As a rule, when it came to women, they held off. As a rule."

"And what happened to Mom?"

He lit his usual cigarette, looked somewhere in the distance, and repeated my last words, pensively. "What happened to Mom . . ."

He and I had never talked about Mom, and in fact I'd never even talked about him with Mom. I realized this just as he launched into the main part of his story.

It was half past eight, and Dad was passing the main university building on the way to his class. He noticed a small crowd, heard excited voices, and assumed it was one of the usual fraternity rituals. These things had never interested him, and he was going on his way when he realized that the designated victim was a girl.

So he went closer to get a better look. The girl, raising her voice, was asking them to let her go, because she had no intention of taking part in this tomfoolery.

The others, all talking at the same time, retorted that it was the rule: she had to pay up. Otherwise—one of them who seemed to be the leader yelled—there would be *consequences*. So saying, he had gestured toward the big fountain. The girl said she would call the Carabinieri, and one of the seniors told her to be careful what she said. Nobody had ever dragged the Carabinieri into the matter of student initiations. The group closed in around the girl. Maybe someone shoved her. She looked as if she was about to burst into tears.

"Hey, what are you doing?" my father said.

"Who the fuck is this?" said one of the gang.

"Someone who wants to play the hero," said another.

"Do you want to end up in the fountain instead of the fresher?" said a third.

"Don't you think there should be boundaries to this nonsense? Maybe including respect for women?"

The nastiest of the group was a short, muscular guy, a medical student who'd been around for years without completing his course, with a crew cut and a prominent chin. He was an amateur boxer, and he enjoyed beating people up, two details my father only found out after the incident. Having a hang-up about his height, he particularly liked to pick fights with people taller than him, and being frustrated by his embarrassing academic career; he liked to let it out on those who were good at their studies. With my father, he could kill two birds with one stone, although he probably didn't know that.

"You think just because you wear glasses, I'm not gonna smash your face in?" he said to my father, giving him a shove.

"Shouldn't you have said: *going* to smash your face in?" He hadn't been able to stop himself from correcting him. The other man looked at my father for a few moments in confusion. Was this thin, bespectacled guy telling him he'd smash *his* face in? It was all a bit complicated for him, so he decided to simplify it. "Take your glasses off, you fag."

My father took them off. He'd never been in a fight in his life. Maybe he assumed the idiot would either back off or just shove him around a bit.

That's not what happened. My father folded his glasses

and didn't even have time to put them away before the brute landed him two punches: one on one side of his face and one on the other.

Why did he do it? Probably because he *could*. Violence almost always depends on this basic reasoning.

One of the punches landed on my father's left superciliary arch and split it.

When the superciliary arch is split, it bleeds a lot, which is why an agitated scene ensued. Some people screamed, some called for help, the frat boys ran away. All my father remembered of that moment, as the world around him lost all clarity (that happens, when you're punched in the face), were two specific things.

The first was the cold spurts of water from the fountain, carried on the wind, that slapped his face and mixed with the blood.

The second was my mother's eyes.

"But did you know Mom before that episode?"

"Only by reputation."

"What do you mean?"

"She was very beautiful. She still is. She was famous for it."

If she was so beautiful, why did you leave?

The words, which, of course, didn't really mean much, materialized unchecked in my head, like a neon sign. They were flashing. Actually, they had been flashing for many years.

"But in the confusion, I hadn't recognized her immediately," he went on.

I took a few seconds to regain contact. "And then?"

"Somebody went with me to the emergency room. I don't remember who it was, maybe an employee from the university, but your mother came too, and waited while they treated me and stitched me up. Then we went for a coffee and a cigarette. Anyway, that's how we met."

"Why haven't you ever told me this story before?"

My father shrugged. "I don't know. It just never came up."

"How old were you?"

"Twenty-one."

"And Mom?"

"Eighteen."

"And you were together from then until . . . well, until you separated?"

A very strange expression came over his face, along with a sad, inscrutable smile. "No. After three years, we broke up."

12

One afternoon—my parents had been separated for a few years—I didn't feel like doing my homework: not an unusual feeling for me. So I decided to make myself a sandwich with whatever I found in the fridge and take a break. The word "break" is a misnomer. That presupposes that something has started and has been temporarily interrupted, whereas I hadn't even started studying. I have to admit, though, that I've never been bothered by such semantic niceties. Even today, I'm perfectly capable of taking a break from a piece of work before I've started it.

The light was off in the kitchen. I switched it on and saw my mother sitting at the table, with her head in her hands and her elbows on the table. She had her coat on, and her bag lay on the floor. She'd been about to go out, but something—a fact, or a thought—had stopped her, confining her in that half-light that was so familiar and yet suddenly so frightening, in a position that wasn't usual for her, with a *look* that wasn't usual for her.

I found the image highly disturbing, and my legs started shaking.

She turned to look at me, in what seemed to me like slow motion, and for a few moments, I almost had the impression that she didn't recognize me. Then she gave a start. "Come here, sweetheart."

I went to her, and she took my hand.

"I'm sorry, sweetheart, I'm so sorry."

"For what, Mom?"

"Sometimes, I don't think I'm up to it; I don't think I'm a good mother. I'm sorry."

It's not true; it's not true that you're not up to it, I'd have liked to tell her.

I'd have liked to tell her that it wasn't her fault Dad had left. It wasn't my fault either; it wasn't our fault. I'd have liked to tell her we'd get through it, even without him.

But I couldn't. Like so many times in my life, I couldn't speak when I needed to. She started crying, and I also started crying and said nothing, and all I could do was hug her, feeling the soft wool of her coat under my hands, and the smell of her skin, smooth and dry, like old, precious talcum powder.

She shook herself out of it and wiped the tears from my face with the tips of her fingers, then told me it was nothing, it was just that there were times she felt discouraged.

They always passed, she said.

She stood up, stroked me, kissed me on the forehead, and said she had to go or she'd be late.

13

There was a kind of ambiguous rhythm to Dad's story. One moment he would seem relieved, even happy that he could open up, as if he'd waited a long time for the opportunity. A moment later, he would appear to be overcome by doubt and grow awkward, almost reticent, and I would be obliged to prompt him.

"I'd really like to hear the whole story," I said during one of these pauses.

He picked up the napkin and carefully cleaned his glasses, although they didn't need it. "We got together a few months after the fountain incident, and we were together for about two and a half years. I was twenty-four and had just been made a regular assistant when . . . well, when we broke up."

"Regular assistant?"

"That was a university post before the reforms. After you graduated, if the professor asked you to work with him, you became a voluntary assistant, which in practice meant that you worked but weren't paid. Then there were competitive exams to become a regular assistant. If you passed, you were hired, paid, and could even perform teaching duties. The next stage was regular professor."

"Which is what both you and Mom are."

"Yes."

"Was it normal to become a regular assistant at the age of twenty-four?"

"Not that normal, but not all that exceptional either."

"When did you become a professor?"

"At twenty-eight."

"And was that normal?"

"Actually, no. Before your thirties, or even forties, it was quite rare."

"And why did you and Mom decide to break up? I mean, as boyfriend and girlfriend."

"I'm not sure it's a good idea to talk about it."

"You were born in nineteen thirty-two, weren't you?"

"Yes. What's that got to do with it?"

"And these things happened when you were twenty-four? In other words, in nineteen fifty-six?"

"Yes?"

"So we're talking about nearly thirty years ago. Something terrible must have happened if you're not sure it's a good idea to talk about it."

That came out well. The tone was sarcastic, but not too much—an appropriate sentence, an adult sentence.

My father nodded, agreeing with me. He lit yet another cigarette, and it was at that moment that I noticed, for the first time, how yellow with nicotine the phalanxes and nails of the index and middle fingers of his hand were.

"All right, the fact is, it's not absolutely correct to say that *we* decided to break up. She was the one who decided, and I went along with it. It was an afternoon in March, a Friday, and we were supposed to be going to the cinema. I still remember what film it was: *The Last Time I Saw Paris*, with Elizabeth Taylor. It was based on a short story by F. Scott Fitzgerald, who was one of my favorite writers at the time. I went to pick up your mother, and she said she'd rather go for a walk because she wanted to talk to me."

He gave a small mirthless laugh and added:

"If your girlfriend or wife changes her plans and says she wants to walk and talk instead, start worrying. You're bound to get a raw deal." He paused for a second or two. "One way or another," he concluded, maybe after considering the various meanings of the words "raw deal."

"What did she say to you?"

"She used a phrase that's rather common in such cases. Though I didn't know back then how common it is."

"What phrase?"

"That she needed a break to give herself time to think. She'd be graduating soon; she wanted to study abroad and was planning to apply for a scholarship. She needed to figure out what she felt and didn't consider it right to keep me tied to a situation that wasn't clear to her. That kind of thing."

"Hadn't you guessed anything? I mean that she might say something like that?"

Another mirthless laugh. "Mathematicians, especially young mathematicians, tend not to notice trivial details like

75

the changeability of the human mind. A long-winded way of saying no, I hadn't guessed a thing."

"And how did you answer her?"

"You know what's strange? I can remember very well what she said—what I just told you—but I really can't remember what I said. I was too shocked; I hadn't expected it. I think I asked her for some kind of explanation, oh, yes: maybe I told her I thought she was making a hasty decision. Stupid of me. Why *hasty*? It seemed hasty to *me*. It was obvious that she'd thought about it a lot; her decision was anything but impulsive. But at the time, I wasn't in a position to make such subtle distinctions."

"And later?"

Dad didn't reply immediately. He frowned, as if trying to reorganize a tangle of confused ideas or wondering how much of it was wise to reveal of that old story. "Hasn't Mom ever talked to you about us?"

I shook my head. It was the answer he had been expecting.

"We split up, as your mother had decided, and I was left with a broken heart."

If somebody had told me, even just the day before, that my father could use an expression like that, let alone use it about himself, I wouldn't have believed it.

"Although you know something? I really can't remember what it was like, having a broken heart. I just have a hazy memory of a horrible, violent emotion. I know it was horrible and violent, because I've so often told myself it was, but I can't recall it."

He suddenly broke off, as if, without realizing it, he had come to the edge of a precipice. He put out his cigarette and didn't add anything else.

But now I wanted to know what had happened next. All at once, it struck me as *urgent*. How come, after splitting up as boyfriend and girlfriend, they'd got back together, married, given birth to me and then decided to separate again, this time for good? What had happened? Who had decided it, that second time? I'd always taken it for granted that it had been my father, but now many beliefs on which I'd based my own sense of identity—who I was, why I was the way I was, and whose fault it was—were losing their solidity, becoming elusive, suggesting other things.

The little scar on his superciliary arch, and his story, had opened a door into hidden rooms. It was impossible to take your eyes away from what was in them, in the semi-darkness. It was impossible to turn back now and pretend that nothing had happened.

"Go on."

He passed a hand over his face in an involuntary gesture. "Too many things happened to tell you about right now. Many aren't even all that interesting, to be honest."

"But how long after that did you meet again?"

"We ran into each other from time to time."

"And when did you . . . I mean, get together again?"

He told me in a neutral, slightly affected way that after a few years had gone by, they had started seeing each other again and within a few months had got married. An account so linear and flat, it seemed purged of its essence.

Just then, Monsieur Dominic came to our table and asked us if everything was all right and if we wanted more brandy. My father said no, thanks, we'd had enough to drink, but he seemed glad of the interruption, as if it had relieved him of the embarrassment of continuing, and started talking to the host. I didn't quite grasp what they were saying, but more or less guessed the subject.

My father asked him what we could do after dinner if we didn't want to go to sleep. The man misunderstood: did we want girls, maybe? I thought I caught the word *putains*, followed by an emphatic question mark. He was a little surprised; we didn't seem the kind. My father smiled. No, no, we weren't looking for girls. We'd like to find a place where we could hear some music, or a cinema that was open until late, or whatever, because we didn't want to go to sleep. Did he have any recommendations? Up until that point, I'd managed to follow. Then they started talking more quickly, and I got lost.

When the conversation was over, Dominic took out the pad on which he noted the orders, wrote something in block letters, tore off the page and gave it to Dad.

We stood up, shook his hand while he said something about the fact that we should come back, maybe even the next evening—or at least that's what I thought he said—and we left.

"What did he write on that piece of paper?" I asked when we were a few dozen meters from the restaurant, going in the direction of the wharf.

"The address of a place where they play jazz. What time is it?" Dad never wore a watch.

"Half past ten."

"He said they don't start playing until midnight. Let's spend another hour or so around here, then go over there."

14

We strolled around the harbor, skirting the borders of the Panier, but not going beyond them.

The area now was almost familiar, a village-like atmosphere strangely combined with a harsh sense of latent danger: something was creeping silently through the side streets, watching us without being seen.

We went into a bar and sat down at a table, though we were determined not to drink any more alcohol. Gastaut had said I should spend two days as a normal eighteen-year-old. Still, we both agreed that the concept of normality didn't include my getting drunk on wine and brandy, even under the close supervision (and with the participation) of my father.

So we ordered two coffees, which were probably the worst of our stay in Marseilles, and started chatting again. I'd never in my whole life taken an interest in anything concerning my father. Now I was interested in everything: the questions just kept coming.

"What were you like when you were my age?"

"I don't know. I've never been able to talk about myself,

I mean, in a reliable way. I think it's a common phenomenon. If you try asking people you know well to describe themselves, you'll realize that almost nobody can do it. In the best of cases, they come out with a few more or less well packaged stereotypes. Or else they tell the lies they need to believe."

"All right, but was there something you really liked?"

"I liked music and mathematics. I dreamed of becoming a jazz pianist and a great mathematician. Of those two ambitions, let's say I've realized half of one."

"What do you mean?"

"I never became a jazz pianist, and I've become, at best, a good mathematician. I fantasized about going down in history for proving Fermat's theorem. I didn't succeed, and, of course, nobody will remember my modest intuitions."

"You'll have to explain to me who Fermat is."

"He was a French mathematician and jurist in the seventeenth century. In past centuries, it was common for the same person to be a jurist and a mathematician. A friend of mine, a professor of civil law, once told me that the intelligence you need to really understand law has a very particular structure that's very similar to that of mathematicians. I was skeptical, so to convince me he quoted a great Polish mathematician, Stefan Banach, who said that good mathematicians manage to see analogies, but *great* mathematicians manage to see analogies between analogies. It's a brilliant definition, and my friend said the same thing holds for jurists: the good ones grasp analogies, similarities and differences, the great ones analogies between analogies. In other words, they're capable of taking the discussion to a whole new level. Anyway, Fermat made a number of important discoveries, but he's become famous over the centuries for a theorem for which, according to him, he'd found a wonderful proof. Unfortunately, he wrote, the margins of the book in which he was making notes were too narrow to contain it. I don't know if he'd really found that proof, in fact, I have my doubts, but since then, mathematicians all over the world have looked for it without success, and even today, nobody knows if it really exists. That's why many people prefer to call it Fermat's conjecture."

"I'm not sure I understand: he made notes in the margins of a book?"

"Yes, in the *Arithmetica* by Diophantus of Alexandria, who was a Hellenistic mathematician."

"And this happened in the seventeenth century?"

"In sixteen thirty-seven, to be precise."

"And since then, nobody's proved the theorem?"

"Some may have got close, but there's still no proof. And remember, apart from anything else, the algebraic tools we have at our disposal today are much more sophisticated and powerful than in Fermat's day."

"Have you ever got close?"

"I *thought* I had, but I was wrong. I tried for twenty years, then gave up: mathematics is a sport for young athletes."

He let a few seconds go by before resuming:

"Somebody will get there sooner or later. For now, the proof has only ever been found in a novel."

"What novel?"

"I've heard that in Oriana Fallaci's latest book—which I

haven't read—the main character discovers the proof, but since he's in prison, in solitary, without paper and pen, he can't write it down, he can't manage to keep it in his head and he forgets it."

"Is something like that plausible?"

My father made an unusual face. "You know, the ways of genius are infinite. Sudden intuitions *are* a fundamental part of scientific discovery, therefore also of mathematical discovery, but let's say that it's highly unlikely for such an intuition to manifest itself if it isn't preceded by a long incubation period, which would, in fact, include a lot of work with pen and paper. Anyway, novels aside, there are many mathematicians who've thought they'd proved the conjecture, then, alone or with the help of someone else, they've realized they hadn't, that at some points of the proof there was an error."

"Why is mathematics so important to you?"

"Because *it was* so important. I've only realized that in the last few years, more or less, since I gave up my attempts to prove Fermat's conjecture. I'd always thought that the reason I loved it was that beauty gave me pleasure. I didn't care at all about the possible practical applications of the things I studied, the things I was trying to discover. The criterion was beauty. Beauty pure and simple."

He took off his glasses, squinted and rubbed his eyes. He made to pick up his cup, but then must have remembered what the coffee was like and his hand stopped in midair.

"Then I realized that, for me, mathematics was also a tool to alleviate anxiety, to fight the stress of existence and its unpredictability—a defense against fear. In German, which is one of the most precise languages there are, with different synonyms for every concept, there's a single word for anxiety and fear: *Angst*. So that's it: mathematics was a defense against fear, a remedy for chaos, and a way to tame it."

He broke off. I think I must have had a surprised look on my face.

"Is everything all right?" he asked.

"I'd never have thought you could tell me things like this."

"Neither of us would ever have thought we'd find ourselves in a situation like this. To stay with the theme of things being unpredictable and out of our control."

"You're right, carry on."

"Many mathematicians like to think—although they don't usually have the courage to declare it explicitly—that everything can be reduced to symbols and formulae. I used to think that myself, more or less consciously: the universe has a mathematical structure, and we just have to discover it."

"And doesn't it?"

"No, it doesn't. Mathematics doesn't preexist the discoveries of mathematicians. It's a construction that explains many things about the world, but not all." He paused again. "Are you following me?"

I was.

"Mathematicians like to feel superior. There's a story, a joke let's say, that describes it very well."

At that moment, a little white dog with black spots, a kind of fox terrier cross, approached us. It let itself be stroked, wagging its tail in a dignified way, as if to show it was friendly but not submissive.

85

"*Tati, viens ici*," cried a lady with short hair, who looked like one of Modigliani's models. The dog ran to her.

"Do you know who Tati was?"

"No."

"A French comedian. He had a surreal, intelligent kind of humor. He died last year." He was silent for a second or two. "Your mother liked him."

The reference to Mom hung between us for a while.

"Oh, yes, the joke. An astronomer, a physicist, and a mathematician are traveling across Scotland by train when they see a black sheep in a meadow. The astronomer exclaims, 'How interesting, in Scotland the sheep are black!' The physicist looks at him with a hint of disgust. 'You astronomers are always making arbitrary generalizations. Actually, the only irrefutable statement we can make is that in Scotland there's at least one black sheep.' The mathematician looks at both of them, sighs and concludes, in a didactic manner, 'I don't know what to do with you two. The only things we can say are that in Scotland there's at least one sheep and at least one side of that sheep is black.'"

It was a good story, I said, in a tone that made me feel adult. It was good, he agreed: it must have been made up by a mathematician—or at most a logician—and accurately reflected the attitude of mathematicians toward other scientists.

He lit another cigarette.

There was something irreparable, something tragic, I thought, in his constant smoking, in that display of a weakness that was almost laid claim to and turned into its opposite. You sensed a deliberate choice to self-destruct in the repetition of those always identical gestures: taking the soft, dented pack from his breast pocket, tapping on the upper edge to push out the ochre filter, putting it between his lips, striking a match, nonchalantly inhaling.

"Sometimes, I think I'm tired."

"Tired of what?"

"When you've lived most of your life in the belief that you're the custodian of a superior knowledge and then that belief shatters, you feel lost. All of a sudden, it seems as if nothing interests you anymore."

"But you have lots of interests; you listen to music, you're a big reader."

"There you are, take reading for a start. It's true; I've always read a lot. But deep down, my attitude was wrong. Dangerously wrong."

"Aren't you exaggerating?"

"Wait, let me finish. I studied, and I read, but in the belief that the really important things were elsewhere. That true knowledge was scientific knowledge, particularly mathematical knowledge, and the rest was just idle chatter, clever at best. I approached novels, or books of philosophy, politics, sociology, in the same spirit in which some intellectuals read detective novels, say, or science fiction. A pastime, not a shameful one certainly, but one whose nature you need to be quite conscious of, especially to yourself, because there are clear hierarchies. There are serious things and there's entertainment, which can be elegant, or sophisticated, or even intellectually complex, but still entertainment. You allow yourself to consume it, but with mental reservations, even if it's an essay by Jean-Paul Sartre. A frivolous pastime of the mind before you get back to serious things. Now, though, I feel as if a chair has been snatched away from under me."

He looked fragile. I had the impulse to squeeze his shoulder, but didn't dare.

He massaged his temples, and half-closed his eyes. "Maybe it's down to the fact that I didn't live up to my expectations, but I suspect that even if my dreams of mathematical glory had come true, I'd have got to this point anyway. I think the simple, banal truth of the matter is that I'm growing old, and I'm afraid of death." He broke off. "I shouldn't talk to you about these things," he added, shaking his head as if in a resolute "no."

"Do you have anyone else you can talk to about it?"

He looked at me, like someone who isn't sure he's understood correctly, who isn't sure he's heard the question. "No, nobody," he said at last.

"Then talk to me about it."

My words appeared to strike a chord with him, almost as if I had given him an inkling of a solution. "All right," he said in a low voice. "I'll talk to you about it." There was no ironic inflection in his voice to suggest the strangeness of this exchange. "I never thought I'd grow old. It seemed to me impossible that at a certain point in my life, I would say, 'I'm forty years old.' Now I'm over fifty."

He finished his cigarette, almost sucking at it, inhaling so intensely that it hollowed two grooves in his cheeks.

"I should have died young. Not physically: I should have died as a mathematician. Changed jobs, let go as soon as I started to realize I'd run out of steam. However good you are—and I was *quite* good—there comes a moment when you discover your own mediocrity compared with superior talent, let alone compared with genius. You should be capable of stopping once you've reached your limit, but that almost never happens."

"When did you realize you had a gift for mathematics?"

The question sounded like a rebuke: I didn't like his argument, didn't like the things he was saying.

He seemed to catch this and adjusted himself; his tone became less bitter. "I was always good at it, even when I was little. But there is a specific episode. One of those moments when you seem to sense a kind of predestination and which it's nice to remember."

"Go on."

"I'd just started middle school. It was in the first weeks of term. The teacher told us an anecdote about a famous mathematician of the past named Gauss: a story about when he was a child. Apparently, one day in Gauss's class—he was nine at the time—the pupils were particularly restless. After a while, the exasperated teacher ordered them to add up all the numbers from one to a hundred. His idea was that they would be kept busy for a while, and he'd have some peace and quiet."

Just then, a hippyish-looking boy and girl my age or slightly older, in sandals and baggy shirts, came up to us, said *Hi brothers*, in English, and asked us if we had a cigarette. My father got out the pack, took three or four cigarettes from it, and handed them over.

"Five thousand and fifty," I said when our eyes met again.
"What?"

"Five thousand and fifty, that's the result of the sum."

"Oh, so I'd already told you the story? I didn't remember."

"No."

"No, what?"

"You never told me the story."

An expression of astonishment appeared on my father's face. "How did you do it?" he said slowly.

I had to think for a moment or two. "Well, I saw the numbers arranged on a segment. All of them, from one to a hundred. Then this segment moved, like in an animated cartoon, and turned into a circle, where the ends, one hundred and one, touched. At this point, it seemed natural to add them together, to make a hundred and one. Then I saw the diameter of the circle, which went from the exact point between one and a hundred to the exact point between fifty and fifty-one. I added them too, saw that the result was the same, and realized that the number one hundred can be divided into pairs whose sum is always one hundred and one. So I multiplied one hundred and one by fifty, in other words, one hundred times fifty plus fifty."

"Are you able to put it into a formula?"

"I think so."

He handed me the little black notepad and the fountain pen he always carried with him and I wrote: $n/2 \ (n + 1)$. Then I changed it to: $n \ (n + 1)/2$.

"That way's better."

I gave him back the pen. He held it in his hand as if it were a cigarette. I was sure that at any moment he would lift it to his lips.

"How much did you get in mathematics in the first term?"

"Six."

"Six. And what will you get at the end of the year?"

"Six."

"Why?"

"Why what?"

"You know what I mean."

I shrugged.

Dad leaned forward. "As a child, in your first years at elementary school, you were very good. Then you moved to middle school, and everything changed."

He had left home when I was in my fourth year of elementary school, and my performance—excellent until then—had gone downhill, so much so that I was almost at risk of failing.

I'd recovered at the start of middle school, settling into a comfortable mediocrity: I did reasonably well in all subjects, I got lots of sixes and a few sevens. But the talent for mathematics I'd seemed to have as a child had vanished.

I looked straight at him again. There was a hint of intense, unbearable vulnerability on his face. I had to look away.

"You didn't finish your anecdote, the one about your teacher in the first year of middle school."

He gave a slight start. "Oh, yes. Obviously, he told us that Gauss had answered after a few seconds and asked if any of us could do the same."

"And you put your hand up."

"Right."

"And what did he say?"

"He asked me how I'd done it. I explained that I'd imagined

the numbers as points arranged on a segment and had added up the ends: one hundred plus one. Then I realized that the sum of ninety-nine and two was the same. After that, it was easy. But your solution is better, with the segment becoming a circle. That's where drawing comes into it."

"How did Gauss do it?"

"We don't know. We don't even know if the anecdote is true or one of the many myths that circulate about geniuses. Anyway, I later discovered that my teacher gave that test to all the first years at the start of the school year. As far as I know, only two of us ever got it right; I don't know who the other one was."

"The teacher must have been pleased."

"He said he would give me nine. In theory, solving the problem in such a short time would have deserved the top mark, he told me, but if he'd given me ten, he would have been implying that there was no room for improvement and would have contributed to making me waste my talent." He thought about this. "I don't remember his exact words, but the gist of it was: never throw away your talent."

15

It was eleven by now.

"So, do you feel like going to that music place?" my father asked.

"Yes, I've never heard jazz. I might like it."

"You *think* you've never heard it. Jazz is everywhere, somebody once said."

"Who?"

He laughed. "Me. But jazz is a subject about which there are lots of sayings. The most famous is by Louis Armstrong: 'If you have to ask what jazz is, you'll never know.'"

He took out the map and looked for the address that Dominic had written on the order pad.

"On foot, it'll take us about forty minutes. We can take a taxi, if you like."

"Let's go on foot; that way, we'll kill time."

"Dominic said it's rather a rough area."

I shrugged. "So was the harbor."

My father made no further objections, and we set off once again along the Canebière. By now, there weren't so many people about, which might have been why some of the neon lights

93

seemed more intense and even, in a few places, endowed with a life of their own.

We passed a porn shop, then another one. As we approached a third one, my father asked me if I wanted to go in.

"Are you joking?"

"If you were on your own or with a friend of yours, would you go in?"

"Yes," I replied, without false hesitation.

"Me too. So we might as well take a look and get it over and done with."

We crossed the threshold. There was a heavy black plastic curtain separating it from the street, beyond which was another world, another dimension.

I remember everything as if I had it in front of me right now. The lighting was harsh and cold, like a morgue scene in a film, and the space much bigger than might have been imagined. From outside, it looked like a small shop, just a few square meters. Once past the curtain, though, you realized it was wide and very deep. There were shelves on the walls, display cabinets along the whole central part, and five or six customers walking about, carefully avoiding each other's eyes. The only employee was a thin, nondescript boy, not much older than me, sitting behind the cash register playing chess with himself.

Videocassettes and magazines were pedantically divided by theme: orgies, lesbians, S&M, gay, whips, animals. The wide range of objects and implements really was for all tastes, and there were oils and creams promising, in four different languages, spectacular increases in size—"up to eight centimeters," it said on a box alongside drawings that left nothing to the customer's imagination.

Now and again, I checked what my father was doing. He seemed at ease, moving between one shelf and the next, examining each thing carefully, almost as if he were planning to write a review of the business and was looking for a starting point. At one point, he picked up a whip—a-cat-o'-nine-tails, to be precise—and tested it by hitting himself gently on the forearm.

At the far end of the room was a line of booths. I went closer to take a look: there was a slot machine next to each door, if you inserted five francs you could go in, choose a film from a vast selection (classified according to subject areas, as on the shelves) and enjoy a private view for a few minutes, with its related privileges.

On each door there was a sign saying: *Prière de laisser cet endroit aussi propre que vous désirez le trouver en entrant.* Please leave this place as clean as you would like to find it on entering.

I was tempted to put in the five francs, but I had only just put my hand in my pocket in search of coins when I heard a series of loud, inarticulate, guttural sounds, like somebody energetically clearing his throat. They were coming from one of the booths and were accompanied by labored breathing in a rapid crescendo that concluded with a rather impressive rattle.

A few moments later, an old man emerged from the booth in question. He stank of cigarettes and was trying to button up his visibly stained fly; it was likely he hadn't obeyed the request on the sign.

I instinctively took my hand out of my pocket and realized that my father was close by.

"Shall we go?" he said in a neutral tone.

We headed for the exit. The chess-playing assistant didn't deign to look at us; I wondered how they managed to check if people were stealing.

For a while, we walked in silence.

"I remember when I was little, you sometimes played the piano," I said. "The one we still have at home."

"Yes, that's right."

"But I don't remember what you played."

"A bit of everything, but yes, mainly classic jazz."

"Did you study music as a boy? I never heard about that."

"I went to a teacher for several years, but I learned to play what I liked only when I stopped taking lessons. In my university years, three friends and I put together a group: piano, drums, bass, and sax. We earned a bit of money playing in dance halls, or at weddings. It was fun. For years we even talked about making a record of our own. Then we graduated, and we each went our way, which didn't involve music."

"Did you compose?"

"Yes, we wrote a few pieces. Two or three were actually quite good, in my opinion."

"How long is it since you last played?"

"Every now and again, I still play a little."

"But where you live, you don't have a piano."

He shook his head, still walking.

"So, how do you manage?"

"I go to a friend who sells them and practice a bit. I always choose a different one."

"Why didn't you take the piano away with you?"

"I don't know. Maybe leaving something you care about in a place you don't really want to leave is a way of staying connected to that place—of hoping to get back there. I don't know."

This left me stunned. If he had decided to leave my mother and me, what did these words mean?

I didn't ask him for any other explanation: I would have had to bring too many things out in the open, and I couldn't. I wasn't ready.

"What kind of music are you interested in?" my father asked.

"I'm not a great fan. I listen to singer-songwriters—some singer-songwriters—rock music, songs that tell a story, or stir your imagination. I'm more interested in the words than the music."

"Give me an example."

I thought this over for a few seconds. "There's a song I very much like. It's by Don McLean. I don't suppose the name means anything to you."

"I have heard it. What's the name of the song?"

"'American Pie.' It's based on something that happened in 1959, a plane crash in which three musicians died. It's full of symbols, and I like listening to it because every time I think I discover a new meaning or a hidden episode. It lasts nearly nine minutes."

"I'd like to hear it," he said, without any condescension.

"Okay, when we get back, I'll lend you the record."

He gave an uncertain smile. "The fact is, I know hardly anything about you. I have no idea what you want, what you'd like to do. But maybe that's true of all parents."

He could not know what I didn't know myself. "I don't know what I want," I admitted. "I've asked myself, and it was like staring into a void. If I tell you something, will you promise me you won't start worrying? It's all behind me now."

"I won't start worrying. I promise."

"I've sometimes wondered how it must be to kill yourself."

He didn't change expression. "In what way?"

"Precisely, that was the problem. I couldn't find a method that seemed sure. I mean: that made me feel certain I wouldn't suffer in any way."

"Do you still think about it?"

"No, not for a while now."

"I've had the same thoughts."

"Really?"

"When I was in high school. Then, one evening, near the end of university, I happened to talk about it with some friends. One of us had taken his final exam and was about to graduate. We drank quite a bit, started confiding in each other, and at one point, I admitted I'd thought about suicide. I thought my friends would be shocked. And in a way they were, but not for the reason I'd imagined. It had happened to all of us, and yet each of us was convinced it was something very rare, something exclusive."

We were silent for a while. There are moments that imprint themselves on our memory indelibly because something happens that changes how we see the world. And it does happen in a moment. That anecdote about suicide jolted me out of the adolescent cocoon I'd lived in until then. The cocoon in which you think your own experiences are unique, indescribable, tragic, and, above all, incomprehensible to anyone else.

"A boy from my school killed himself a year ago."

"I know, I remember."

"Really?"

"I'd have liked to talk to you about it, but I didn't know how. Did you know him well?"

"No, only by sight. We'd played soccer together behind the school a couple of times."

"Did they ever find out why he did it?"

I opened my arms wide. "Nobody could figure it out."

"There are short-circuits in people's minds and souls that nobody will ever manage to pinpoint. Trying to explain them you could go mad." He took out his cigarettes again.

"Do you think you should smoke that much?"

I blurted this out, surprising even myself.

He looked at me for a few seconds. Then he put the pack and the matches back in his pocket.

We had come to a crossroads. My father stopped to look at the map. There was nobody around.

"This way," he said, pointing to a street on our left. "I think we're nearly there."

16

Block after block, the city had changed. Now we were in a half-deserted area on the outskirts with a few cars parked here and there. There were yards full of weeds and refuse, nasty smells, ghostly boarded-up buildings, housing estates that seemed uninhabited with the odd dim light in the windows, tall dilapidated fences behind which disused warehouses could be glimpsed. Over it all, there hovered a sense of desolation and neglect.

A small pack of dogs crossed the street, a sheepdog cross at the head of the procession, the others following in a disciplined single file, in a kind of choreography that reminded me of the sleeve of *Abbey Road*. They disappeared one by one into a side street, fading into the darkness, and a few moments later, I wondered if I had really seen them.

"Are you sure this is the right place?"

He showed me the map. The name of the street we were crossing corresponded to the one Dominic had written on the piece of paper. "It should be this way, but it's definitely a strange place for a music venue."

"I'm taking this anyway," I said, picking up a rusty iron

bar, the kind used in reinforced concrete. He appeared about to say something—don't do anything stupid, leave that thing, something like that—then must have thought that, considering the surroundings, arming ourselves wasn't a completely mistaken idea.

We kept on walking. A taxi drove past us and stopped a hundred meters farther on. Three people got out and walked in somewhere, while the taxi moved away quickly, as if the driver didn't want to stay in the area a minute longer.

"Maybe it's there," I said.

"I think it is," my father said, going nearer.

The half-closed gate led to a yard at the far end of which was a low building with a green and purple sign: *En Fusion*. I threw away the iron bar, and we approached. Some cars were parked near the building, and in front of the entrance stood two forbidding-looking men. One was tall and fat, with the smooth face of a depraved buddha; the other was his opposite: thin and dark, with muscular arms that looked like leather ropes. Neither of them looked like people you would want to get into an argument with.

They asked us if we had an invitation. My father said, no, we didn't have an invitation, we didn't know we needed one, but Dominic from Chez Papa had suggested we come, to hear music.

The mention of Dominic worked. They exchanged looks; the fat man, who seemed to be in charge, nodded. The thin man asked us for a hundred francs each, didn't issue any tickets, and let us through.

It was a large space with not much light and a lot of people:

wide-open windows, a smell of cast iron, smoke, and bodies. On one side, there was a bar with a wooden counter and saw-dust on the floor all around; on the other, up against a wall of timeworn bricks, a bandstand onto which the musicians were climbing at that very moment.

Dad lit a cigarette. "Strange place, isn't it?"

"Yes, it is."

"I'll have a drink, but maybe it's best if you . . ."

"Me too. Gastaut said I should do everything a normal eighteen-year-old would do, and we have to follow doctor's orders."

My father raised his hands in surrender. We went to the bar and ordered two cocktails—Perroquets, they were called—made with pastis, green mint syrup, water, and ice. The kind of cool, pleasant drink you knock back, like certain drinks you had as a child, and which, before long, muddles your brain and makes your legs shake.

I looked at the people. They were all older than me, but there were lots of girls. Some were young, and some were beautiful, and some wore tight skirts or trousers, and were cheerfully vulgar, and I wondered what might happen during that infinitely long night I had in front of me and on all the other nights of my new life—because I was thinking then that I would have a new life—and I told myself gleefully that I was feeling good and that not sleeping wasn't so bad after all, maybe you could learn to do without it, because that way time would become much longer and much more interesting.

The musicians on the bandstand alternated. Every quar-ter of an hour, the drummer or the saxophone player or the bassist or the trumpeter changed. They were all men, apart from a girl who played the drums for a while with wild eyes and an expression that seemed to hide a secret guilt. Only the pianist stayed the same: a guy in a white shirt, a black tie, and a gray Borsalino pulled back to leave his forehead uncovered. Before every piece, he would light a cigarette, inhale a few times, and let it burn itself out in the ashtray, the smoke describing lethal curlicues in front of his face.

It was a jam session, my father explained.

"That's when musicians get together to play without a prearranged program, sometimes without even knowing each other, and take turns improvising on standards."

"What's a standard?"

"Right. A standard is . . . how can I put it? . . . a really famous jazz piece that, over time, has become a classic, something that everyone knows. A theme, a kind of musical grid to improvise on. A framework."

A table became free just in front of the musicians, and we went and sat down at it. My father was right: I thought I'd never heard jazz, I mean, I'd never heard it deliberately, but in among the dissonances, the solos, the give and take, the quotations, I did recognize something.

He seemed happy; I can't find a less banal word to describe it. Whenever they launched into a new piece, he would mention the title and the composer. Then he would listen rapt, keeping time, nodding his head at the most successful passages.

Now there were four people playing: piano, drums, bass, and trumpet. The drummer had long gray hair tied in a bun and kept looking around as if searching for someone who wasn't there. He was sweating a lot, and now and again would wipe his face with a towel.

The guy who was playing the bass was tall and handsome, looked straight ahead, and seemed shy. He had his arms around the instrument like a bridegroom hugging his bride in an old photograph.

The trumpeter was a black man in his fifties, with pock-marked skin and eyes expressing terminal boredom: nobody knows the things I've seen, and I don't want to talk about them anyway. He was there, but he didn't give a damn. He didn't give a damn about anything, except the music he was playing, the notes that rose and fell languidly and painfully and hypnotically while he closed his eyes and the veins on his neck swelled and it seemed as if he and his trumpet were in search of an idea hidden somewhere in the air, in search of a secret rule, the key to everything.

My father was drumming on the table with his open hand and tapping with his foot on the floor. He was looking at the musicians—actually, he was looking mostly at the trumpeter—and a vague smile hovered over his lips.

"I don't know anything about it," I said after a while, "but I get the feeling the one playing the trumpet is the best."

"He is. The others are playing quite well, but he's the one who really has intention."

I was about to ask him what he meant by intention, but he went on:

"The piece is called 'So What,' it's by Miles Davis. One of the greatest musical geniuses of this century. Actually, we can leave out 'of this century.' One of the greatest musical geniuses of all time. Someone who changed the history of music."

Just then—or maybe later, but our minds tend to adjust memories, to give them more meaning and order than the events to which they refer actually had—a guy got up on the bandstand and approached the pianist. He whispered something in his ear, and the pianist picked up his glass from the floor, stood up, apologized to the other musicians, bowed slightly to the audience, lowered his hat over his forehead, and walked away to a smattering of applause. The others stopped playing while the same guy who had spoken to the pianist turned to the audience—us—and asked if there was anyone who wanted to play the piano.

Nobody stepped forward, so he repeated the invitation two or three times, without success.

My father shifted on his chair, as if he'd had the impulse to stand up but then had thought better of it and told himself: don't do anything stupid, Professor, let it go.

"Do you want to go up?" I asked under my breath.

"No, no, better not," he replied under his breath.

"Why better not? I mean, if you can do it, why not go?"

"Better not," he said again, keeping his eyes fixed on the bandstand and the empty piano stool.

"Go," and, without even realizing what I was saying, I added, "I'd love to hear you play."

He turned slowly toward me and looked me in the eyes to see if he had understood correctly. Then he nodded, stood up, and waved his hand to attract the attention of the guy on the bandstand.

As he walked to the piano, I suddenly felt scared that he wouldn't be up to it. As a young man, he had played at weddings and student parties, and now he practiced from time to time on borrowed pianos; in other words, he was an amateur at best, and maybe I'd sent him up to make a fool of himself in front of these unknown French people who would have no qualms about booing and humiliating him.

Why hadn't I kept quiet? I asked myself. I sucked the melted ice at the bottom of my glass through the straw, feeling that something irreparable was about to happen.

Dad sat down, immediately stood up again and adjusted the stool, tried a couple of chords, stretched the muscles of his neck, looked down at the keyboard, and tried again. Then he raised his head and looked at the other musicians, one by one.

"'So What,'" the trumpeter said. "*Ça va?*"

"*Ça va*," my father replied, and they started playing without saying anything more.

At first he was cautious, wary. I didn't know much about music, let alone that particular kind of music, but I had the impression he wasn't playing enough notes, that he was a little tense, that he was feeling his way, trying to get in sync with the others, searching for a point of entry.

Then, gradually, the keys seemed to free themselves. The sounds of the piano appeared to become fuller and richer, and he launched into a dialogue with the others, like somebody politely joining in an already started conversation.

I was watching his every gesture in a state close to anguish: it was all so alien to my image of him, so mysterious.

There were times when he closed his eyes, times when he

swayed back and forth. His hands were nimble, rapid: their movements conveyed a sense of simplicity that was very beautiful, like a well-managed metaphor, an ideal of style, a way of being in the world.

They had been playing for about ten minutes, and the trumpeter was in the middle of a solo, when the pianist in the Borsalino reappeared at the side of the bandstand. He stood there, listening and smiling. My father saw him and nodded in his direction as if to say: okay, I've seen you, I'll hand it over to you now. The other man replied with a gesture as if to say: keep playing. My father smiled.

The trumpeter noticed this—so he wasn't as absent as I'd thought—launched a series of conclusive notes, turned in the direction of my father, and gave way to him. "Go on, it's your turn," said the simple, measured turn the pockmarked black man made with his body, with his head, with his trumpet: a sign of respect for the amateur pianist who'd had the courage to get up on the stage and play with them.

And Dad played a solo. I would never have admitted it to myself, but I was really proud of him and wished I could tell everyone near me that the tall, thin, elegant-looking man sitting at the piano, looking much younger than his fifty-one years, was my father.

When he finished, summing up the meaning of what he had played in two conclusive, melancholy scales, there was a burst of friendly applause. And I also applauded and kept doing so until I was sure he had seen me, because I was starting to realize that there are such things as misunderstandings and I didn't want there to be any at that moment.

In the years to come, I would listen to a fair amount of jazz in its various manifestations and forms. I would learn concepts I knew nothing about that night in Marseilles: variations, paraphrases, dissonance, clusters, chromaticism, interplay, modal improvisation, free jazz.

But all I really understand about jazz—however much or however little—I learned that night.

17

We decided to go back on foot, the way we had come. We could have called a taxi, but we told each other that if we wanted to kill time, it was better to walk.

"Kill time, what a stupid phrase," my father said. "We don't need to kill it, it passes by itself; it doesn't need any help from us."

"I sometimes think about these set phrases and wonder where they come from. Some are really absurd. The cat's whiskers, for example. What does it mean?"

"I used to know, but I've forgotten."

"It's a phrase I've always hated. Maybe because a teacher in middle school who I hated was always saying it."

I saw the iron bar I'd left on the ground when we arrived, and after thinking about it for a few seconds, I picked it up.

"Just to be on the safe side."

As before, he didn't say anything—this time without even thinking about it.

"I read a good phrase about the passing of time," he said, kicking a plastic bottle.

"What was it?"

"It got late, very early."

I laughed, although I wasn't old enough to fully understand the deadly accuracy and truth of that short phrase.

"I never would have imagined you played like that," I said after a few blocks.

"I was shit scared when I sat down. But luckily, it didn't go too badly. It was one of my favorite pieces."

"I didn't even think I'd like jazz."

"And did you?"

"Yes, I did, although I couldn't explain why."

"The nice thing about jazz is its imperfection. Imperfection in the etymological sense of the word."

"I don't know what you're talking about."

"Perfect comes from the Latin *perficere*, to do something completely. Imperfection, in the etymological sense, is that which isn't complete. Incompleteness distinguishes jazz from any other kind of music. In classical music, for example, the score contains all the notes to be played. The performer reads it and plays the written notes, nothing less but also nothing more. His performance is all about the many different ways he can interpret those notes, but the notes are always the same. In jazz, the score is just the starting point."

"Does that have to do with what you told me earlier about standards? That there's a grid that the musicians improvise on?"

"That's right. You start with the standard, in other words, with the notes written in the score, and then you go off in search of other things. Other things that you don't know before you start. The player is also the composer of the piece he's playing."

"You said the man on the trumpet had *intention*. What did you mean?"

He lit a cigarette and slowed down a little as he walked, as if to concentrate and collect his thoughts. "Well, that's one of those concepts where St. Augustine's words about time are valid: if nobody asks me, I know. If I try to explain to someone who asks me, I no longer know."

He finished his cigarette before he resumed speaking.

"Let's put it this way. Your intention is where you want to get to when you're playing a piece. Or rather, to be more precise, it's *where* you want to get to but also *how* you want to get there. It's the destination, but also the route. There may be many kinds of intention: serious, dramatic, frivolous, or clever or witty. I can't explain it any better than that."

"The trumpeter seemed very serious."

"He *was* very serious."

We passed a guy in pajamas with a big mastiff on a leash. Man and dog looked at us suspiciously: it was obvious we didn't belong in this place, so what were we doing there in the middle of the night?

Speaking of time, I looked at my watch and wondered if he was taking the dog for its last walk of the night or its first of the morning.

"How are you?" my father asked me after another few blocks.

"Fine. And you?"

"I'm fine too. I don't feel tired at all."

It was two-forty, we were walking quickly and were both wide awake and in a good mood. In a way, I was starting to grasp the mysteries of the city in which we had been moving for many hours now. It was as if I sensed its hidden spaces, its secret lives, the windows where people's silhouettes passed for a moment and disappeared forever. I glimpsed, in the broken lines of those streets, the hidden code of my present life and above all my future one.

Dad's eyes were slightly blurred, his expression intent but also light.

"What do you think? Are we lost?" I asked him.

"I think we are."

"Shall we check the map?"

"What does it matter?" he replied with a hint of care-free madness in his voice. "After all, we don't have any commitments."

I looked at him for a few moments to see if he was being serious. He wasn't being serious, but nor was he joking, I concluded.

"Somebody said that losing your way in a city doesn't mean much, but getting lost in a city the way you would get lost in a forest is something you have to learn."

So we tried to learn how to get lost. Before long, we were gripped by an inner fever: we were thinking differently, see-ing things—inside and outside ourselves—we would never otherwise have noticed.

"Sometimes I wonder what it really means to be free," I said out of nowhere.

"I don't think there's such a thing as freedom without a

certain element of risk, of insecurity. Freedom is an uncertain balance, it's being a little out of place."

"I like the idea of feeling out of place."

"Your mother and I said that, many years ago."

Then several minutes passed in which all that could be heard was the slight whistle of his smoker's breath, the muffled noise of the occasional car that passed us and disappeared, the sound of our footsteps.

"It looks like there's a bar open over there," I said, seeing a lighted sign in the distance.

"Let's go and have a coffee."

"Okay."

"But leave that thing outside," he said, pointing to the iron bar, which I was now carrying casually, like a service weapon. "If we get into an argument, it might be better to trust our dialectical talents."

18

The place wasn't welcoming. The light was cold and harsh, and on the walls were posters of soccer players from both Olympique Marseille and the French national team and other posters of guys in shorts and boxing gloves kicking each other in the face, with the words *Savate championnat national français 1981*, or something like that; on a high shelf, next to the posters, a number of cups were on display.

Behind the filthy old wooden counter with its marble top was a man my father's age, who looked like a slum version of a Hanna-Barbera character, a slightly surly Ranger Smith with a three-day stubble. On one side of the interior, there were a few metal tables, which must once have been blue.

At one of these, three guys were sitting. In front of them, they had little glasses containing an amber liquid; they were smoking big unfiltered cigarettes and arguing in loud, animated voices.

Seeing us, they fell silent for a few seconds. My father asked the barman if we could sit down, and he nodded and, in an obvious effort at politeness, even gestured with his hand toward one of the free tables.

We ordered two coffees. The barman asked if we also wanted a splash of pastis in them. My father thought about it and said it was better not, adding that we had to stay awake. For some mysterious reason, Ranger Smith liked this answer and even almost smiled.

"Dad, I was thinking: I'm the one who has to stay awake. Why don't we go back to the hotel and you sleep a little? I'll read, I feel fine."

"No. If I don't keep an eye on you, you might fall asleep too, and we'll be back to square one."

I was about to say something in reply, but he continued:

"And anyway I don't feel like sleeping. I like staying awake. I've always thought of sleep as a duty. Being given permission to do without it gives me a sense of freedom."

There wasn't much to add, so I changed the subject. "Then we need to decide what to do tomorrow, or rather today, in just a few hours."

"What time is it?"

"A quarter past three."

The barman brought us our coffees and asked us if we were Italian. We said we were, and he immediately became friendlier. He told us his grandfather was from Sorrento, his name was Gerard Iaccarino, and even though he was born in Marseilles and had never been to our country, he felt half Italian. He spoke a hybrid language that even I managed to understand.

The previous year, in the final of the World Cup, he had supported Italy, after Germany had stolen the game from France on penalties in the semi-final. The best player in Italy, in his opinion, wasn't Paolo Rossi, but Claudio Gentile, and Italy had won the cup because it had the best defense in the world.

"What kind of sport is that?" I asked, pointing to the posters with the men in boxing gloves kicking each other in the face.

Savate, he replied. A sport born in Marseilles. It was like boxing, but you could also use your legs. One of the guys on the poster was his son, who'd come second in the French championships in 1981.

Four young men came in talking excitedly over each other, as if something had just happened that they had widely divergent opinions about. Gerald Iaccarino went back to his place behind the counter.

I don't remember how we ended up talking about sex, but after a while, I asked my father if I could ask him a personal question.

"Go ahead."

"A *very* personal question."

"If it's *too* personal I'll tell you I don't feel like answering it."

I liked that answer. Except that now I actually had to ask that very personal question. And formulating it out loud wasn't easy.

"I was wondering . . . I mean, I wanted to ask you how old you were when you were with a girl for the first time."

He took a deep breath. He let ten seconds or so pass, maybe even more.

"I was nineteen," he said at last, but his expression suggested he hadn't finished his answer. We were silent for a while.

I had never talked about this subject with my friends. Some, like me, had never been with a girl. Others had, and I was embarrassed to ask them what it was like, how you were supposed to behave, and all the rest. I was afraid I'd look like a loser; I was afraid of being made fun of; I was afraid they might think of me as a pathetic failure who at almost eighteen hadn't yet been with anyone, who asked morbid questions and masturbated like a thirteen-year-old.

After a rapid calculation, I realized that if it had happened when Dad was nineteen, it hadn't happened with my mother. This made the conversation less difficult.

He resumed, as if he had reorganized his thoughts:

"Almost all my friends had already been with a woman. I was one of the few not to have had the experience."

I'd never imagined that, in my father's time, so many had already done it by the time they were nineteen. There are lots of clichés, I told myself. We always think that in our parents' day, most people didn't experience sex for real until they got married. Basically, that everything was less free.

"Were you together? Was she the same age as you?"

He gave a slight smile. I thought he was going to take out his cigarettes and light one, but he didn't.

"It wasn't so easy, at the time, for someone . . . for a girl to have complete sexual relations before marriage. For men it was different: there were always whorehouses . . . brothels."

It was obvious, but it had never even remotely crossed my mind. The thought that my father had been with whores struck me as inconceivable. In reality, I couldn't even imagine it after those words: even just the linguistic possibility of putting my father together with the word "whore" was absurd.

"Does that make you uncomfortable?"

I was about to lie, then told myself it would be a lack of respect, a way of going backward from the unexpected point we had reached.

"A little. To be honest, I hadn't expected it."

"Well, it'd make me uncomfortable too. And it did make me uncomfortable for a long time, having done something like that. Before it happened, I used to say it would never happen. Afterward, I wondered for a long time how it had been possible."

"But how did it work? I mean, did you just go to one of those places, knock on the door and go in? What did you say? I'd never have summoned up the courage. I never would, I think."

"I thought the same thing. But then some friends took me. They told me it was normal, necessary, in fact, because that way, I'd learn, and I wouldn't run the risk of making a fool of myself when I ended up going with a woman I wasn't paying."

Silence fell. The next thing would have been to tell the story. But maybe we weren't ready for something like that. Maybe we never would be.

"How was . . . I mean, what was she . . ."

"She was normal. A bit fat, but normal. She looked like the caretaker of the apartment block next to mine. She looked so much like her that for a few moments I thought it actually was her. The whole thing lasted three or four minutes."

This time he did light a cigarette, and after a few puffs, his features relaxed a little.

"For a long time I thought that, if I could only turn the clock back, I wouldn't have gone to that brothel. I was filled with longing for that first time I'd never had, something I could have remembered with tenderness instead of with shame. A lot of times we don't realize that the things we do for the first time are points of no return. For good and above all for ill. If they're wrong, nobody will ever give them back to us."

He finished his coffee and smoked.

"You know, I'd never have thought of telling this story. Let alone telling it to my son."

"Did you ever tell Mom?"

"A few months after we got together—the first time, I mean—the conversation happened to get round to brothels. There was a big debate, in parliament and in the county, about the possibility of abolishing them, which did, in fact, happen later, in nineteen fifty-eight, I think. Your mother was full of contempt for brothels, for those who ran them and especially those who visited them."

"I can just see her," I laughed.

"She said that a man who goes with a prostitute is either a lowlife or inadequate. Or both. I tried to say that was a bit simplistic, a bit too *tranchant* . . . Lots of men, for generations and generations, had had their sexual initiation—let's call it that—with an older woman. A governess sometimes, or indeed a prostitute. Did that mean that all of them, generation after generation, were lowlives or inadequate, or lowlives *and* inadequate?"

"What did she say to that?"

"Obviously, there was no way, not just to convince her, but even to get her to soften her position. You know better than I do how severe she can be in her judgments. Anyway, at the end of the conversation I said, as usual, that she was perfectly entitled to think the way she liked, but that to me it seemed perhaps a bit too drastic—you needed to see shades of gray—I didn't like the idea of women's bodies being treated like merchandise either. Still, I didn't share her extreme views—things like that. Basically, I tried to maintain my position, but I couldn't wait to change the subject. I don't think I would ever have told her about my experience anyway. But that conversation made it impossible to ever bring it up."

I knew what he meant. Especially when it came to certain subjects, Mom didn't go in for shades of gray and could be very harsh. I was well aware of that, and yet the way Dad was telling me this story offered a new perspective, not only on him, but on him and her. On the balance—or lack of it—in their relationship, the power struggle between them.

"Antonio."

"Yes?"

"Don't tell her the story. I don't want her to know."

"I'd never do that."

"I know, but I thought I should say it anyway."

If a week earlier—or even two days earlier—anyone had told me that my father had been with a prostitute, I would have been disgusted. Now, though, I couldn't work out my feelings about that revelation. I felt a mixture of surprise, curiosity, and something like tenderness.

I was very confused, and he had fallen silent. Then I realized that he was waiting for me to reciprocate, to tell him something about me.

"I've never been with a girl, I mean, I've never had complete sex. Sometimes I think it'll never happen."

"It'll happen soon, and then your current worries will seem very strange." He lit a cigarette. "Have you ever smoked?"

"I've never touched a cigarette. When did you start?"

"We all smoked when we were kids, including loose cigarettes."

"How do you mean?"

"You didn't have to buy a whole pack. You could go to a tobacconist and ask for, I don't know, five cigarettes, and he'd put them in a thin white paper bag. That lasted until the sixties; then loose cigarettes were banned because they said it encouraged young kids to smoke. Which was true."

"Have you ever tried to quit?"

He smiled, ignoring the question. He was thinking about something else.

"I've never really liked any other woman since your mother," he said as if resuming a conversation he'd interrupted a long time ago.

19

One day, I'd heard my parents talking about a colleague of theirs, a university professor—an important one, a rector, or a dean—who had left his wife for a female student.

You know those occasions when adults talk, convinced that the children can't hear them, and that even if they do hear them, they won't understand what they're talking about? As children, all of us have listened to at least one conversation like that, so we should know how it works. Instead of which, once we've become adults, we forget it and think children are deaf or stupid, and we let them hear and understand—or misunderstand—things we'd rather they didn't hear and understand. Let alone misunderstand.

That conversation made a big impression on me: a man of fifty, in other words, quite a bit older than my father at the time, had got together with a young woman of twenty-five.

I knew that professor: he and his wife had come over for dinner several times. He was a short, round, aloof man with a little beard streaked with gray and glasses with thin frames. For some reason, I took a great dislike to him. If I'd been able to categorize him according to age, from my point of view as a child at elementary school, I would have said he was almost an old man: someone closer to my grandparents than my parents.

The main thing I thought I understood from what Mom and Dad were saying, while I pretended to read a Spider-Man comic, was that a couple might separate and divorce, but that it wasn't right for a university professor to get together with one of his students. It wasn't the first time, and it wouldn't be the last, my mother said after a while in a conclusive tone. That was the concept that stayed with me, a kind of revelation of how things go in the world: very grown-up men—let's say almost old men—university professors in particular, leave their wives for their students; that's wholly reprehensible, but unfortunately, it happens with some frequency.

Two years or so later, my father moved out.

Everything happened in quite a civilized way: Mom and Dad summoned me into the dining room and told me there are times when a husband and a wife, even though they love each other, feel the need for a break so that they can be alone and have time to think.

"You mean you're getting a *divorce*?" I asked, trying to overcome my panic, during a pause in the flow of words with which they had filled the silence of that October afternoon. The word "divorce" had always struck me as mysterious and slightly disturbing. Exotic. Something that concerned other people in other places.

They shook their heads almost in unison and launched into a subtle—and for me at the time, incomprehensible—disquisition on the differences between *divorce* and *separation*.

They weren't getting a divorce. They were just taking a break; well, let's say it was a temporary separation in order to overcome certain difficulties. But I mustn't worry, as far as I was concerned, everything would stay the same. Dad was going to be in a different place for a while, I would stay with Mom, but I would be free to go and see him whenever I wanted, I would be free to stay with one or the other depending on what I wanted, and so on. I would be free.

The substantial legal differences between the institutions of divorce, separation, and a break were rather lost on me.

What wasn't lost on me, though, was that my mother and my father were telling lies, that things *wouldn't* be the same and that, when it came down to it, my father was leaving, just like his colleague with the little gray-flecked beard and the glasses with the awful frames.

Which meant he was leaving my mother—and me—for a student of his who wasn't much more than twenty. I was sure of this from the very moment that discussion in the dining room ended, even though there was no clear evidence pointing to it. Actually, the fact that they hadn't mentioned any specific reason for this break convinced me that there was such a specific reason but that they didn't want to tell me. And they didn't want to tell me because it was something improper, even shameful.

Because of that, I started to harbor an unspoken hostility toward my father. But also toward my mother, for a different and complementary reason.

He had done something wrong, something immoral; she, on the other hand, had done something inappropriate and annoying: she had behaved in much too civilized and compliant a manner. He had left, performing an act that she herself, sometime earlier, had considered inadmissible, so how could she be so calm, so accommodating? She should be getting angry; she should be making him pay, she should be getting him to feel how unfair his behavior was.

Not even for a second, in the weeks, months, and years that followed, did it ever cross my mind that my interpretation was simply the fantasy of a child made angry and unhappy by the break-up of his family.

It didn't matter a jot that, over the years, I didn't find in my father's little apartment any clue, not just that another woman was living there, but even that one had passed through. This lack—I thought with fanatical conviction—pointed to the precautions they were taking not to be found out.

With adolescence, and with what happened to me, I stopped thinking about my father's phantom girlfriend, but my hostility toward him didn't disappear. I simply stopped being conscious of it; it became a simmering resentment, a background murmur in my mind, something you only become aware of when it suddenly ceases, giving way to silence or a different sound.

My father's words—"I've never really liked any other woman, since your mother"—uttered that night, in that bar, in some vague part of a strange city, didn't square with what I had always imagined about my parents' separation.

20

We left the bar at about four-thirty, after trying the hot, buttery croissants that had just arrived from a nearby bakery.

We asked Monsieur Iaccarino to explain where we were and what direction to take to get back to our hotel. If he wondered how or why we had ended up in this area, he didn't let on. He pointed out the way—if I'd trusted to my intuition, I'd have gone in exactly the opposite direction—telling us that on foot it would take us at least three-quarters of an hour. If we wanted, he added, he could try to call us a taxi, but he wasn't sure it would come to this address.

We said no, thanks, we could do with the walk, we said goodbye and set off.

The air outside was cool, almost biting. Every now and again, passing old, half-open front doors, we were hit by whiffs of mildew, damp, and urine.

"I see you don't step on the manhole covers," my father said after a while, smiling in the semi-darkness.

"What?"

"You avoid the manhole covers. I used to do that too when

I was young, and I was on my way from home to university for an exam."

He was right. It was a habit I'd picked up—I didn't know why—a few years earlier; by now, I did it without thinking. I thought of it as a secret personal eccentricity, one of the many ways I thought I was different from other people.

"Why?" I asked.

"For the same reason as you. A little private superstition, most of us have them. There are those like us who avoid manhole covers, and those who deliberately step on them, but taking care not to touch the edges. Then there are those who stay away from the curb, those who walk only on the unpainted part of pedestrian crossings, and so on."

"And when you went to your exams . . ."

"I avoided the manhole covers. Sometimes I'd tell myself it was absurd, actually a worse superstition than the ones about black cats, nuns, or spilling salt. I'd tell myself it was unworthy of a rational, mathematical mind like mine. And yet for four years, I never stepped on a manhole cover on the way from home to university on exam days: I was too worried that something unpleasant might happen, and I didn't want to run the risk. Anthropologists call it 'magical thinking.'"

"Magical thinking?"

"Yes, it's the mental mechanism by which we see meanings where there aren't any, imagine non-existent relations of cause and effect and convince ourselves we can influence reality through our thoughts or through symbolic or ritual acts. Magical thinking is the principle behind belief in the evil eye or lucky charms. I don't know if I've explained it well."

"No, I understand. I don't walk under a ladder because I believe it could bring bad luck, but between my passing under the ladder and any bad thing that might happen, there's no relation of cause and effect, except in my imagination. It's all in my head."

"Congratulations. We all have superstitions. There's a wonderful story about Niels Bohr, one of the greatest scientists of all time. Apparently, he'd put a horseshoe on the front door of his house in the country. One day a student paid him a visit and was astonished to see that horseshoe. 'Professor, do you really believe a horseshoe on the front door brings good luck?' 'No,' replied Bohr, 'of course I don't. But it seems to work anyway.'"

He seemed pleased to be able to tell me anecdotes and explain things. Above all, he seemed pleased by the fact that I was letting him. It hadn't happened since I was a child.

As the sky started to get lighter, the streets started to fill up. People running, workers with sleepy faces and little shoulder bags with their lunch, bakers' boys delivering bread, street sweepers, policemen, nurses, as well as survivors of the night hurrying back to their lairs before the light of day turned them to ash. One of them spat as he passed us and gave us an indecipherable smile.

My father and I had stopped talking and had been walking at a good pace for about ten minutes when I had a sudden, dizzying, twofold sensation, one I'd never had before and have only had a few times since. I felt part of a multitude and, at the same time, was able to gaze down at it, as if from the top of a tower.

People, more and more of them as dawn advanced, swarmed through streets and alleys and avenues and squares, joining and dividing and describing shapes in perpetual motion, like some flocks of birds in the sky. All of us, my father and me, the street sweepers, the workers, the louts, the policemen, the nurses, the criminals, the bakers' boys, the down-and-outs, formed a single giant organism of which I alone was conscious.

By the time we got to the hotel, it was already day. The elevator was out of order, the doorman told us, they'd be coming to fix it at about seven-thirty. Our room was on the fourth floor. We walked up. By the time we got to the landing, my father was out of breath, and for a moment or two, I got scared. Then it passed.

"This is where we have to be careful," he said, throwing the windows wide open onto apartment blocks turning pink in the early morning light.

"Careful?"

"We have to rest a little, but we mustn't fall asleep. Go and have a shower and take one of those pills."

I did as I was told. The warm water was pleasant, and when I finished, I took the pill, even though I said I didn't need it, because I felt fine and had no desire to sleep, and I was impatient to go out again to see what adventures the day that was starting had in store for the two of us, my father and me.

While he went to have a shower and a shave, I took out my Walkman and one of the mixtapes I'd made especially for the trip. I can still remember the playlist, the way we remember the members of the soccer teams we supported when we were kids.

"Romeo and Juliet," "Private Investigations," "Ragazzo dell'Europa," "Should I Stay or Should I Go," "Under Pressure," "Caterina," "Always on My Mind" in the version by Willie Nelson.

I lay down on the bed, put on the headphones, and pressed play.

I don't know what song was playing when my eyes closed, I only remember my father in his bathrobe, shaking me gently by the shoulder.

"So, you didn't need a pill, eh?"

"I wasn't asleep. I was listening to music . . ."

"Sure, and I was lifting weights. Go and have another shower, and make it cold this time. Then we'll go out and have breakfast and work out a program for the day."

21

After breakfast, we went back up to our room to rest a little. Lying on the beds, but awake.

"I've studied the guidebook," my father said.

"Yes?"

"Apparently, the one thing we mustn't miss is Notre-Dame de la Garde: it's the church we could see from the harbor, the one at the top, all lit up, I don't know if you noticed it. Apart from the building itself, there's supposed to be a wonderful view of the city and the islands. Then we absolutely have to see the *calanques*."

"What's that?"

"The *calanques* are geological formations: a whole lot of inlets and cliffs just outside Marseilles. You can take a boat from the Vieux Port and make a three-hour trip. What do you think?"

I yawned deeply and stretched. I felt quite good, and the pill had started to take effect. "Okay, where do we start?"

"We can take a taxi to Notre-Dame de la Garde, visit the church, and enjoy the view. Then we go down to the harbor and find the quay and the ticket office for the tour of the *calanques*."

Half an hour later, we were in the taxi; my father chatted with the driver throughout the ride. Among the things I was discovering about him was an unexpected chattiness, a readiness to talk to people and take an interest in them. I wondered if he'd always been that way, and I'd never noticed, or if it was an effect of the bewildering situation we were in.

They spoke rapid, impenetrable French. I understood almost nothing of the conversation, apart from the fact that the driver was originally from Brittany, that he hated the *beurs*—the children and grandchildren of North African immigrants— who'd taken over the city, and that he would leave Marseilles if only he could.

Notre-Dame de la Garde was a building of impressive dimensions, all in marble, neo-romantic in style, located at the highest point of the city. It was half past eight; the air was limpid, the whole of Marseilles was at our feet, the sea glittered in the distance like a promise.

"Over there are the Frioul islands," my father said, consulting the guidebook and pointing to a little archipelago very close to the Vieux Port. "On the smallest of them is the Château d'If."

It took me a few seconds to focus on the place and the name. "You mean the one in *The Count of Monte Cristo*?"

"Yes. It was a prison up until the beginning of the century."

"I didn't know it actually existed. I thought it was an imaginary place."

"No, it exists. The novel actually starts there."

The Count of Monte Cristo, which I had read twice, first in an abridged version for children then in the complete version, was one of my favorite novels. I liked stories of adventure, injustice, and revenge, I identified totally with them, and the one I liked most was that one, the story of Edmond Dantès. In the voracious, distracted way I read, though, I had never lingered over the fact that the novel was partly set in Marseilles, the actual place where I was right now. I felt an exhilarating sensation, as if all at once I'd been given the opportunity to visit Smallville, or Toontown, or Gotham City.

"It's a pity we don't have a camera," I said, looking in all directions at the view.

"Yes, it is. But who'd have thought we'd need one?" my father said, and the words imprinted themselves in my mind as if they were a mysterious maxim, a prophecy.

We wandered around the church, looked at the giant statue of the Virgin on the bell tower, studied the city from every angle and when we'd had enough—after a while, even the most beautiful views start to cloy—we took another taxi to get down to the Vieux Port.

At the stand where you could buy tickets for boat trips to the *calanques*, there was a round woman with large, very conspicuous breasts and a friendly expression. She spoke in a slow, pleasant way, carefully articulating the words, and I understood almost everything. After tearing off the tickets, she looked us up and down and asked if we had bathing costumes. No, we didn't, my father replied. Why? Was it also possible to go bathing? Of course it was, she replied. The boat would take us to small beaches where there was very clear water—more beautiful than in Corsica, she said with a hint of pride—and it would be a pity to waste the opportunity.

If we liked, there was time to go to a nearby shop she could point the way to and buy what we needed.

So it was that we went and equipped ourselves with bathing costumes, slides and beach towels. We also bought a cute bag decorated with fish and seahorses.

We were on our way back to the quay when all at once, my father stopped.

"What is it?" I asked.

He was smiling in a strange, ambiguous, almost surprised way. "You know something?" he said. "I'm enjoying myself."

Those words broke my heart. All I could do was give a vague smile and nod my head. "Me too," I said, and it was true. I had never enjoyed myself so much in my life.

There were ten or so people on board, apart from the boatman, a tall, broad, bearded guy with tattoos on his forearms. There was a French family—father, mother, and two silent children—and a group of German women tourists all dressed up as if they were going for an excursion in the woods. We changed in the boat's small cabin, putting on our Marseilles bathing costumes with a degree of pride. The sea was calm, with very slight ripples on which the sunlight produced a constantly changing glitter that, for some inexplicable reason, made me think of eternity.

"Who'd ever have thought there were such beautiful places in Marseilles? Practically in the city," my father said after we'd been sailing for half an hour, observing the white and ochre cliffs plunging vertiginously into the sea. He was wearing dark goggles over his usual glasses, a device that went back to the days when acquiring graduated sunglasses was a luxury. With such an old-fashioned accessory, his white shirt, and his bathing trunks, he looked like a character from a sixties film.

He was right. The coast was breathtakingly beautiful. The intense blue of the sky drew, for whoever was capable of seeing them, upside-down shapes that wedged themselves between the pointed tops of the cliffs. Some rocks seemed to defy the force of gravity: huge boulders atop edges or points, in perfect but precarious balance, like the images in some cartoon films. High up, gargantuan, primordial caves; down below, giant crags that slid like ramps all the way down to the sea.

In the distance people could be seen lying in the sun, although it wasn't clear how they had got there, because there was nothing behind them but steep cliffs. My father asked the boatman, who replied that there were paths, but you had to know them really well because they were steep and dangerous, and more than once, inexperienced hikers had fallen from the cliffs to their deaths.

In some places, we passed so close to the walls of rock that we could touch them with our hands. They were hundreds of meters high and aroused an almost religious sense of reverence.

We had been sailing for more than an hour, and the sun was beating down when we entered a small *calanque* where the sea was green and transparent. The boatman cast anchor and said that whoever wanted to could bathe.

We dived in from the stern, almost simultaneously, feetfirst and holding our noses with our fingers. The water was cold and clear, and we swam together as far as a little beach of pebbles and gravel. We turned back when the boatman waved at us, signaling that we had to leave again.

I had been a small child the last time my father and I had been to the sea together.

The *calanque* of Morgiou, which was bigger than the others, had a marina with boats and a little fishing village. My father asked if we could take a walk on land. The boatman replied that it wasn't part of the schedule, but if we liked, he could let us off, and two hours later, we'd be able to catch the next boat. He would inform his colleague that there were two people who needed picking up.

So he dropped us at the landing stage, we waved goodbye without any regrets to the other passengers, with whom we hadn't exchanged even a word, and headed for the village.

The place seemed almost uninhabited, even though there was a little bar open. We went in for a coffee, and the owner pointed out to us the path that would take us in five minutes to a little beach where, he said, the sea was magnificent, and there was almost nobody around. My father asked him how far Marseilles was by land, and he replied, with a touch of pride, that this *was* Marseilles, ninth arrondissement. That didn't mean you could go on foot all the way to the center: the Vieux Port was about fifteen kilometers away. But we were in Marseilles. We wouldn't find a sea like this, he concluded, in any other city in Europe.

We followed his directions, climbed for a few minutes, and came back down onto the beach.

"Wow, it's really beautiful," I said, looking around.

There were only five people on the beach: three very sweaty young men with rucksacks and beards, who had obviously arrived there by land, and two women who had set up camp—with folding chairs, a cooler, and even a table—in the shade of a pine that grew out of the white rock five or six meters higher up.

There was all the space we wanted, so we spread our towels on the stony beach, about ten meters from the two women; the men were at the other edge of the beach, and the silence was almost unreal. Chalky rocks fell sheer into the sea almost everywhere, dotted with pines and scrub in many shades of green.

In the distance, the steep paths the boatman had told us about were just visible. From time to time, tiny human figures walked along them, emerging from the scrub and venturing precariously above the drop.

We spent an hour going in and out of the water while the sun climbed ever higher in the sky, growing increasingly hot. Eventually, my father said it was best to be in the shade for a while in order to avoid getting sunburn. So we took our things, moved to where the two women were, under the Aleppo pine, and asked for permission to sit down near them.

One of the two replied in passable Italian, "You'll have to buy a ticket."

We looked at her, both taken aback.

Still quite calm, she went on, "You have to give me a cigarette; otherwise, you can't sit here." Then she burst out laughing. "I'm trying to quit, so I don't buy them. But I saw you smoking, and I got this terrible craving." She motioned to us to sit down next to the two of them.

The other woman now joined in, saying something in French and laughing, although in a reproving tone.

Dad also laughed and held out the pack to the one who'd spoken first.

"What did she say?" I asked.

"She said her friend has quit smoking, but only her own cigarettes."

We made ourselves comfortable. My father placed the pack with the lighter between our towels and their chairs and told them to help themselves whenever they liked; they didn't need to ask.

"How come you speak Italian?" he asked.

"I lived in Florence for a year, just after university. I taught French and learned Italian. How come you've ended up here?"

We gave an incomplete version—a very simplified one, let's say—of the facts and asked them if they were from Marseilles. No, they were from Toulouse, they were here for a week, staying with a friend.

Their names were Adèle—the smoker of other people's cigarettes—and Lucie. Adèle seemed older, possibly about forty, and was the more beautiful of the two, although the other one had something opaque about her—a hint of lazy sensuality in her gaze—which made it hard for me to take my eyes off her.

They were architects and had spent years designing or renovating houses, but neither of them had liked it. Then, almost as a game, they had started writing and illustrating stories for small children. They had been successful: their books had been translated into other languages and, after a while, they had realized that they could afford to give up architecture.

The nice thing about their work, Adèle said, were the long periods of free time. They produced three books a year, each one took about two months' work, so the arithmetic was easy. Every year they had more or less six months' holiday to devote themselves to whatever they wanted, especially travel.

The main thing, she explained as if she were imparting a lesson (which was in fact what she was doing), was not to work any more than you had to, maybe only putting enough money aside for emergencies.

"An informed thriftiness," my father said, nodding, and it struck me that I should remember this, that when I came to choose my life's work, I should bear these words and this encounter in mind.

"Are you hungry?" Adèle said after a while.

We were quite hungry, as it happened.

From their cooler, they took some ham and cheese sandwiches, some cucumbers and a bottle of white wine, and together we feasted cheerfully, chatting like old friends.

We were drinking coffee—they had also brought coffee in a thermos—when about two hundred meters from us, on an invisible path at the top of the cliff, a line of hikers appeared as if from nowhere.

The scene reminded me of a film I'd seen a few years earlier at the school film club, a film that had had a great effect on me: *Picnic at Hanging Rock.*

It was based on a true story, apparently, of a group of Australian schoolgirls who in 1900, during a school trip, ventured up the rock and went missing. Only one of them was ever found again, in mysterious circumstances, and she had lost her memory and was unable to say what had happened.

It was a disturbing, poetic film about fate and the fundamental mysteries of life, youth, and death. "Everything begins and ends at exactly the right time and place," said Miranda, the almost celestially beautiful protagonist, who, for a long time, I couldn't get out of my head.

Just as I remembered those words, one of the hikers missed his footing and plunged down a gravel escarpment. He managed to stop only very close to the cliff edge, from which there was a drop of at least fifty meters to the sea.

It was a terrible, unreal scene. The man tried to climb back up, but the escarpment was too steep, and his companions seemed not to know what to do. Their voices were indistinct, muffled by the distance.

I thought with dismay that I was about to witness someone's death and was overwhelmed by the enormity of what was happening. All around, nature was peaceful and very beautiful, exactly as it had been a few moments earlier, exactly as it would be later.

The rescue operation was laborious, and it wasn't easy to make out the details. The fallen hiker's companions threw him a rope. Then, cautiously, to avoid falling themselves, they slowly pulled him up onto the path. He hadn't hurt himself, not seriously at least, because they all set off again and before long disappeared behind the cliff.

Adèle took another cigarette, and this time Lucie also asked for one. All three of them smoked in silence because nobody was ready to speak. Their cigarettes were still alight when the boat we were supposed to be going back on sailed into the *calanque*.

"There they are, we have to go," my father said, getting to his feet.

"Why go?" Adèle asked.

"Our boat has arrived."

"Stay, it's the nicest time of the day."

"We'd love to, but we wouldn't know how to get back."

"We'll give you a lift. We left our car in the village. We'll take you straight to your hotel, the full service."

I was about to reply immediately and say yes, but I held back, not wanting to look like a little boy. I had the distinct impression that my father had also been on the point of answering immediately. He too held back. He turned to me. "What do you think?"

"Come on, let's stay. We're fine here; we don't have any commitments until tomorrow morning."

So we stayed there for another two hours at least, chatting about this and that—Adèle was very impressed on discovering that Dad was a mathematician—drinking coffee, bathing in the sea, and watching the sunlight fading and changing the colors of the *calanque*: from white to ochre to gray in all its gradations.

At one point, Lucie, in her very labored Italian, told me I looked like a young actor in the Comédie-Française.

She said a name I'd never heard and immediately forgot.

Before I could think of an intelligent reply, Adèle intervened, laughing. She said that Lucie had just given me a compliment, because that particular actor was a very handsome young man.

We got back after six, going along the Chemin de Morgiou, a wild road like something in the mountains, passing the prison of Marseilles, which, they told us, housed the worst criminals in France, and driving through anonymous, inhospitable-looking residential areas.

"What are you doing tonight?" Adèle asked us when we were almost at our hotel.

"Nothing," my father replied. "Looking for somewhere to have dinner."

"There's a kind of party at our friend Marianne's house. Why don't you come? There'll be some interesting people there."

This time my father didn't ask my opinion. He immediately said yes, great; we'd love to come. So when we said goodbye outside our hotel—*à tout à l'heure*, Dad said, *à tout à l'heure*, I repeated—we had a note with Marianne's address and an agreement to see each other again in a few hours.

At a party. My father and me. In Marseilles.

22

"Do you want to go to the party?" my father asked me when we were alone.

I was desperate to go to it, but I thought I ought to get a grip, so I replied rather nonchalantly, "Yes, sure. The night'll pass more quickly."

"Then before we go up to our room, let's find a shop where we can buy a couple of bottles of wine, we don't want to show up empty-handed. They'll be closing soon, so let's get a move on."

We walked a few blocks without speaking. I could feel the salt stinging my skin, and I was a little dizzy from tiredness and excitement. My father, on the other hand, seemed in great form, he'd caught the sun, and you wouldn't have known that he'd spent a night without sleep and hadn't rested at all the following day.

"Pretty, weren't they?" I said, when I realized that he hadn't mentioned the subject.

"Yes, they were."

"Do you like Adèle?"

"She's an interesting woman, very pleasant to talk to. That doesn't happen often."

"How old are they, do you think?"

"Adèle more than forty, Lucie thirty-five, I'd say."

"And what do you think? Is Adèle trying it on with you?"

He burst out laughing. As if I'd suddenly cracked a good joke. "It might be fun, but they're lesbians," he replied, continuing to walk.

Lesbians? I hadn't noticed anything, and if he was right, I'd been barking up the wrong tree entirely in my imagination—about Lucie in particular, and about what might happen that evening, at the party. It shook me.

"Why lesbians?" I asked, my voice unwittingly rising a couple of tones.

"I may be wrong, but the way they looked at each other, the way they treated each other, they didn't seem just friends. Also, the way their movements were in sync, which is something you sometimes see in couples who've been together for a long time. For example, at one point, Adèle adjusted a lock of Lucie's hair; it had fallen over her face, and she moved it behind her ear for her. It was a very intimate gesture. But like I said, I may be wrong."

I didn't know what to say. I asked myself if I'd ever met a lesbian couple before. I told myself I hadn't. Which might mean two things: either I really hadn't met one or I had and simply hadn't recognized it for what it was.

How was it possible, though, that my father had noticed these details? He'd always struck me as distracted, uninterested in people, focused only on his world of abstract symbols.

Now I was discovering, among other things, that he was capable of catching and interpreting details like a hand affectionately rearranging an unruly lock of hair.

Just then we came to a general food store, with a big old window with dark wooden frames, in which all kinds of good things were displayed: cold meats, cheeses, sweets, salmon, herring, bottles of wine, bread, chocolate, preserves.

The grocer was wearing a white apron, beneath which he wore a shirt with an impeccably knotted dark tie. He was a friendly man—a characteristic of Marseilles people, as far as I could see—and he recommended two bottles of Châteauneuf-du-Pape. The wine was produced about a hundred kilometers from Marseilles, and that particular cellar was of great quality. We wouldn't have to spend an excessive amount of money, and we'd look really good.

"Have you ever read anything by F. Scott Fitzgerald?" Dad asked me on our way back to the hotel.

"Yes, *The Great Gatsby*. Why?"

"As the grocer was talking about the area around Marseilles, I remembered that one of his novels is set in this part of France."

I didn't say anything, because I hadn't understood where he was going with this. Nor did he, I realized a few moments later: he looked like someone searching for the lost thread of what he was saying or thinking.

"Nothing, it must be the lack of sleep. I keep making strange connections between things and then immediately forgetting them. Anyway, the novel is called *Tender Is the Night*. Beautiful title."

"Yes, it is. And the story takes place here?"

149

"On the Côte d'Azur, but at the beginning they mention Marseilles. Right now, I can't remember why."

"I liked *The Great Gatsby* a lot."

"Fitzgerald was a great writer and an unhappy man. There's a sentence of his I often think about: 'In a real dark night of the soul it is always three o'clock in the morning.'"

These words and their poetic rhythm fixed themselves in my mind.

It was a perfect insight, and at the same time, it seemed to me to contain the opposite of its surface meaning, as happens to the best metaphors, beyond the intention of whoever created them.

"You take a shower first," my father said. "Cold, please, that way, while I'm having one myself, I won't have to worry that you'll fall asleep."

I stayed in the shower for at least five minutes and came back into the room, still dripping, with the towel around my hips. The window was open, and my father was on the balcony, smoking; the air was cool and made my wet skin shiver. For a few suspended, wonderfully absurd moments, I had the thought that my father and I could move here and live just as we were now, without rules and without a break.

When he went into the bathroom, I took my pill and sat down outside with my book.

I wanted to read a little, but soon realized that I was having a few problems doing that. I didn't understand the meaning of the sentences; I stumbled over single, perfectly normal words and couldn't grasp their meaning, as if the book were written in a foreign language. Then it struck me that the balcony was starting to spin around me, I began to feel nauseous, and I heard the beating of my heart, more intrusive than it had been for years.

I thought, "I'm about to have a seizure. I have to call Dad and get him to take me straight to the hospital. Right now."

I tried but couldn't speak, let alone call out. I couldn't do anything. I was there on the deck chair with the book lying on my lap, the towel covering my hips, and I couldn't speak, I couldn't even move.

But I was thinking frantically. What had that seizure four years earlier been like? I couldn't really remember it, I had lost consciousness, and later I had woken up. As far as I knew nothing had really happened, it had been like a sudden nap. Maybe, when it came down to it, epilepsy was an almost harmless thing. Or maybe I was dying. I thought it just like that, without a question mark: maybe I'm dying. I contemplated the idea very calmly.

"Antonio, are you all right?"

It took me a few seconds to recover contact with the outside world. "I'm fine. I just felt dizzy."

"Is that all it was? You looked as if you were in a trance."

I felt myself—my arms, my chest—tentatively. "No, that's all it was. I mean, I was really dizzy, it must be the lack of sleep, but I feel better. How about you, any problems?" The panic I had moments ago subsided.

"I'm feeling dizzy too. Before we have dinner, let's have a strong coffee. You've already taken your pill, haven't you?"

We sat there on the balcony in silence, resting for half an hour. We watched as the sky filled with clouds, white at first, then gradually darker and more compact, and it occurred to me that it might rain and how lucky we'd been with the weather and all that sun and maybe we should take a taxi to get to the party and my father was a much more surprising person than I would ever have imagined and when we got back home I wanted to keep talking to him because he said interesting things and I had the impression we had become friends and this was strange but great and what a pity it was that Lucie was a lesbian because I'd liked her a lot and I'd had the impression—absurd, I know—that she liked me too.

Yes, I'd recovered from that momentary turn, but there was still a certain elusive quality to my thoughts, the ideas and images chased one another, flashed past and went away before I could grab hold of them.

It was a feeling that was both pleasant and disturbing, and it lasted until we were out on the street again, and the pill started to take effect.

We were wearing white shirts and had the bright, shiny color of people who've spent the day by the sea.

The Canebière now seemed to us to have an almost domestic atmosphere, even though it was the same street that had scared us just two evenings earlier. Now we felt part of the human ebb and flow moving in camouflage into the night.

After a few hundred meters, I realized that I could *hear* people talking on the street. They were talking in Arabic—*I assumed* it was Arabic—or in French, or in French and Arabic together, building up a collective whisper, a frenetic murmur, sometimes friendly, sometimes mocking and dangerous.

Not even for a moment did I think that, if all went well, this was my last night in Marseilles.

Adèle had written the address for us, along with directions on how to get there.

"The Panier isn't as dangerous as they say," she'd said as she gave us the piece of paper, "but it doesn't hurt to be a bit careful."

In fact crossing the border—Quai du Port—separating the harbor from the old city, where we hadn't yet been, we became aware of something different, like a feeling of being watched and, at the same time, a different level of identification with the city and its less accessible nooks and crannies.

In some places, there were piles of rubbish. On a corner, we saw the carcass of a moped from which the seat and all the wheels had been removed. Very young boys, almost children, moved around in groups, appearing and disappearing from the side streets; the lighting was unstable, as if it had just been restored after a long period of darkness; from the entrance halls of buildings came strong smells of food and humanity.

We got to Montée des Accoules and climbed it to Rue du Refuge, where Marianne's apartment was located, in a block from the Twenties or even earlier, with shutters that must once have been green and plaster peeling in places. There was something both temporary and final in the facade of the building and, thinking about it, in the whole of the old quarter. The front door was open.

The apartment was on the ground floor, at the far end of a badly lit entrance hall. We had to use the knocker, as there was no bell.

After about twenty seconds, the door opened, and we made the acquaintance of Marianne.

23

"*Vous devez être les italiens. Je suis Marianne,*" she said, holding her hand out to my father, who replied with a smile, introducing himself in his turn.

Then Marianne turned to me and looked at me for a few seconds, almost as if she were finding it hard to categorize me. Finally, she held out her hand to me too.

She was wearing glasses with masculine-looking black frames and thick lenses that didn't lessen even slightly the impact of that ironic gaze, those dark eyes, those long, dangerous eyebrows.

"*Je suis Antonio, je ne parle pas français,*" I stammered.

"*C'est dommage*, you should do something about it. What about English?"

Yes, I replied, I knew English. More or less.

"You should still learn French, though. Anyway, tonight we'll speak Italian. That way, I get to practice and if I make mistakes, you can correct me."

My father handed her the bottles, she thanked him, said we shouldn't have, but Châteauneuf was always welcome, and asked us to come in, because we couldn't continue the conversation in the doorway.

"Tonight, we're celebrating the arrival of Adèle and Lucie from Toulouse. They're my best friends, but you already know them. On that side, there's food, on the other the drinks. Help yourselves and make yourselves at home. I hope you like North African food."

We had come straight into a large open space: more like a converted warehouse than the living room of a traditional apartment. The air smelled of something I didn't know, a kind of sweet incense, and the walls were a watery green color; up against the left one was a long narrow table with two candlesticks at the ends and the food; against the right wall, a rough wooden chest with another candlestick and the drinks. Chairs, a sofa on a rug in front of a TV set, large cushions on the floor, a shelving unit full of books and objects, a stereo propped up on the floor, about twenty people walking around and chatting.

"I'll go and put down the wine, I'll see you in a bit," Marianne said, walking away. It was all too clear, I thought, that she didn't need to practice her Italian, let alone to be corrected.

"All right," my father said. "Let's look around and try this North African food."

"Have you tasted it before?"

"Yes. When it's good, it's very good."

We separated to inspect the place independently of each other.

At the far end of the living room was a French window that looked out onto a courtyard with plants in large vases and chairs where some of the guests were eating, drinking, and smoking; it should be said that it was a really mixed, really varied human collection.

There were two bearded guys in almost sleeveless T-shirts with muscles like laborers—they actually looked like laborers, or dockhands—holding hands and gazing at each other lovingly; a diaphanously thin blonde girl who was eating like a carter; a small group of young guys, some white, some black, not much older than me, standing in the farthest part of the courtyard: everything—from their movements to the smell—suggested that they were passing around a sizeable joint.

What drew my attention more than anything else was a man in his sixties, in jacket and tie, who looked a lot like Marty Feldman. The resemblance was so strong that after a while, it crossed my mind that in a situation like this, anything was possible, so it wouldn't have been at all strange if it really was him. I had almost decided to introduce myself and ask for his autograph, congratulate him and tell him that *Young Frankenstein* was the funniest film I'd ever seen in my life when I remembered that Marty Feldman had died the previous year; I had heard it on the TV news.

The kitchen also looked out on the courtyard, and had walls painted ochre, like in a Van Gogh. A short black woman with a determined, or even decidedly ill-tempered expression, was busy at the oven.

I went back inside and noticed that over the main door were some words: I went closer to read them. They had been painted on the wall in a fine, slightly childlike cursive hand; I liked the effect of the black writing on the watery green wall. What it said was: *Le merveilleux nous enveloppe et nous abreuve comme l'atmosphère; mais nous ne le voyons pas.*

"Hi, Antonio, you came. I'm glad." Adèle had materialized behind me. She hugged and kissed me as if we were old friends who hadn't seen each other for ages. She smelled of shampoo and body lotion, and seemed wired, as if she had already had a few drinks and maybe smoked something. Everything, thinking about it, seemed a little wired. Lucie also arrived, she also hugged and kissed me, and despite what my father had told me, in contact with her skin, I felt something turn upside down inside me. For a few seconds, I had a dizzying, specific sense of the improbability of the situation in which we found ourselves, like being intoxicated, or in a dream.

"Do you understand what's written?" Adèle asked me.

"More or less. Not all the words. Does it mean that we're surrounded by wonders and don't realize it?"

"Excellent. So it's not true you don't know French. Go and get something to eat, you must be hungry, there are some very nice things"—and she and Lucie slipped away again.

I did as she had said: I took a plate, filled it with everything I could lay my hands on—couscous, salad, pancakes—poured myself a glass of wine and joined my father, who was sitting eating on the sofa.

"It's a strange situation, isn't it?" he said with a flash of slightly twisted joy in his eyes.

"There isn't anything that's not been strange in the last two days," I replied, filling my mouth with chicken couscous.

"You're right. We'll have a few stories to tell."

These words gave me a sudden, brief feeling of sadness. Imagining that we would tell other people what was happening to us implied that everything was over, whereas I didn't want it to be over, I wanted to stay suspended at the point where I was, on the borderline, the exact point between before and after.

A large tabby cat suddenly appeared, and curled up between us, without any shyness, as if we were regular guests in this apartment, and it knew it had nothing to fear. After a few seconds, it even started to purr, sounding like a diesel engine at low speed.

"It's the Cheshire Cat," I said.

"The Cheshire Cat?"

"The cat from *Alice in Wonderland.*"

"I didn't remember that's what it was called."

"That's the name they gave it in the Disney film."

"Ah, now, I understand. Hi, Cheshire Cat," he said, in the serious tone of a madman. He gave it a friendly pat on the head, which the cat showed it enjoyed by half-closing its eyes, then emptied his glass and lit a cigarette.

We sat there on the sofa, the three of us, I don't know for how long.

Now and again, I would get up and go and fetch some wine for both of us; now and again, he would get up and do the same. Without overdoing it but with a certain regularity, so to speak.

Everything was gently disorientating. The people moving around us, those who came and sat on the sofa—it was very large—and then got up again, those who were outside or looked in from other rooms in the apartment seemed like genial shadows, friendly entities devoid of physical consistency.

Dad and I talked, but I had the distinct impression that both of us were finding it hard to keep up the thread of the conversation. At one point, I saw Adèle and Lucie, amid the shadows, exchanging a quick kiss on the lips.

"You were right," I said. But he hadn't seen the kiss and didn't know what I was referring to, and I didn't explain.

It started raining, and the guests came back in from the courtyard, but the living room was large, and there was space for everyone. I was trying to string together some coherent thoughts and not succeeding. From time to time, I would feel dizzy, and for a few moments everything would spin around me like a roulette wheel. Then things would slow down and stop, and I would feel as if I'd reached a new level of consciousness or unconsciousness.

Without realizing it, I found myself staring at one of the candlesticks: the wax was melting, dripping, forming stalactites. Some were about thirty centimeters long and reached all the way down to the table. There was a mystery hidden in those shapes, I told myself, but I couldn't grasp it. Everything had become hard to grasp. In fact, it had become hard to keep my eyes open, and the desserts arrived in the nick of time, just as I was about to fall asleep. There were nougats, almond doughnuts, a cake made with very thin puff pastry, and a soft sweet cut into squares that looked like the quince jam I'd had as a child.

I was eating some almond and sesame nougat when Mari-

anne appeared in front of us and sat down on the rug, leaning
a hand on my legs. It was a very casual gesture, very natural
and yet—in my now confused and altered perception of what
was happening—also very deliberate.

"My friends tell me you're a mathematician," she said to
my father.

He nodded and smiled. Maybe he was about to say something, but his rhythm had slowed down, he didn't answer in
time, and she turned to me.

"And you, Antonio, what are you studying?"

I replied that I'd be finishing high school the following
year, and she looked surprised. She'd thought I was already
at university. I looked older. That made an impression on me,
because I'd always been convinced I looked younger. Just then,
two women and two men approached: they were leaving and
wanted to say goodbye to her. When she stood up to kiss them,
I noticed she had a tattoo on the inside of her forearm, a kind
of mythical animal with wings, an eagle's wings, I think, and
the head of a lion.

These days, having a tattoo is quite normal, almost com-
monplace. It wasn't back then. Back then, only a few categories
of people had tattoos: artists, crazy people, hippies, some bikers,
and ex-prisoners.

I had no idea what Marianne did for a living. She didn't
seem to belong to any of these categories. Maybe she was an
artist; I had to ask her now that she again sat down with us
after saying goodbye to her friends who were leaving. What
had become of Marty Feldman? I couldn't see him anymore.
Had he left without saying goodbye?

I worked out one sentence after the other in my head, giving them a complete, elementary shape, as if I were talking to someone who wasn't very intelligent. I was doing it to give a modicum of coherence and consistency to my thoughts, which were now running away from me in all directions.

"Antonio?" My father's voice was slow and distant. "Are you all right?"

"I have to go and rinse my face," I said, making a huge effort, first to speak, then to stand up.

The walls of the bathroom had been painted sky blue. I liked it that a different color had been chosen for each room, I thought that when I had a place of my own, I'd do the same. I threw a lot of water on my face, but it wasn't enough, so I put my head under the shower.

As I was tidying my wet hair, I don't know why, but it occurred to me to open the medicine cabinet. It contained the usual things: aspirin, mouthwash, bottles and jars of unknown medicines, peroxide, a couple of ointments, and a box of condoms.

That sight disturbed and embarrassed me, and woke me up more than the cold water. I closed the cabinet, left the bathroom and went back to the living room.

"Everything all right?" Dad asked me.

"Yes, everything's fine."

"Your hair's wet."

"I'm fine."

"The others are leaving, what shall we do?"

"It's raining; maybe we should wait for it to stop."

Marianne came back with a drink and a cigarette and sat down in front of us again.

"My favorite moment when I have a party at home is when almost everyone has gone, and there's time to talk."

"How come you speak such good Italian?" I asked her.

"I lived for a long time in Palermo and in Reggio Calabria."

"Why Palermo and Reggio?" my father asked.

"I'm an anthropologist. I study the similarities between primitive tribal cultures and criminal communities. Among these, of course, there are the Mafia-type associations in the South of Italy: Cosa Nostra in Sicily and the 'Ndrangheta in Calabria."

That was very interesting, my father said, and if he hadn't been so tired, I'm sure he would have asked to hear more. But it was obvious that he was finding it hard to keep his eyes open and his thoughts connected.

"I haven't asked you why you're in Marseilles," she said in a light tone. My father was about to reply, to tell her, I assume, about our holiday in Provence or something like that.

I got in ahead of him and told her the real reason we were in Marseilles, the reason we were there that night. I kept it short, but didn't leave anything out. I don't know exactly why I did it, it came to me instinctively, and afterward I thought I'd made the right choice. I felt good. I felt alert and clear. I felt like a man.

Dad didn't show any sign of surprise at what I'd said; rather, I was aware of a sense of relief, a relaxation of tension in his face.

"So, this is the second night in a row you haven't slept?"

"Yes."

"And if you hadn't come here tonight, what would you have done?"

"We'd have wandered around the city, like last night," I replied.

"With this rain, that would have been quite a problem," my father cut in. "So we're really grateful for your hospitality. But now it's best if we go." He was speaking in slow motion.

"If you go, what will you do if you can't sleep? Apart from the fact that it's still raining. Stay here. I'll make coffee, you can rest, and when day comes, you can go back to your hotel."

My father tried to say something in reply, but she told him to be quiet and not get up from the sofa. She said it in just the right way, humorous but at the same time serious.

"I'm just going to say goodbye to some people, and then I'll be right back."

24

I can't rule out the possibility that I may have fallen asleep for a few minutes.

My next memory is of Marianne and me sitting on the carpet next to the sofa. My father, though, isn't there, and the guests all seem to have left. Now the scene has the texture of a dream.

"What is it meant to be?" I ask her, referring to her tattoo.

"It's the opposite of a gryphon," she replies.

"How do you mean, the opposite?"

"A gryphon has the body of a lion and the head of an eagle. This one, though, has the body of an eagle and the head of a lion."

"And why did you want it like that?"

"I don't know. I often do things for the pleasure of feeling original. It's a childish attitude, but I can't get rid of it."

"It's beautifully drawn."

"It was done by someone who lives near here. He was in prison for ten years: that's where he learned to tattoo."

"Aren't you scared to live alone in an area like this?"

"For me, it's the safest place in Marseilles, they're all my friends. I can come back alone, at any time, without any problem."

I look around. "Are we the only ones left?"

"Yes."

Just then, my father comes back. He must have been to the bathroom, and I don't know why, but I hope he didn't look in the medicine cabinet. He sits down again on the sofa, where he was before. The Cheshire Cat isn't here anymore; I have no idea where it went. Through a door I haven't noticed before, Adèle and Lucie emerge. They're both wearing long T-shirts over bare legs; they're ready for bed. We say good-night, they kiss us, they seem to take it for granted that we're staying—maybe Marianne has told them everything—then they disappear again behind the same door.

"Let's make the coffee," Marianne says to me. We stand up, and my father makes to follow us. "Stay on the sofa," she says to him. "Rest, maybe sleep a little."

"I can't," Dad says. He looks really exhausted now.

"You can. Don't worry. I'll look after Antonio."

"What time is it?"

"Nearly three."

Dad thinks about this for a few seconds and decides he can trust her. So he stays where he is, or rather makes himself more comfortable, while we move to the kitchen.

"I have a moka pot that I bought in Italy," Marianne says. "Or would you prefer a French coffee?"

"I prefer Italian, thanks."

"Of course, stupid question. I needn't have asked."

She makes it, and we drink together, sitting at the table.

"I'm sorry I've kept you awake," I say.

"I don't have any commitments tomorrow; I'll sleep when you leave."

"I don't understand why you're concerned about me."

She thinks this over for a while. "Maybe for the same reason as the tattoo, in other words, for no reason. Or maybe because your situation is *balikwas* and I like the idea of being part of it."

"What did you say?"

"*Balikwas*. It's a word in Tagalog, the main language of the Philippines. It's not easy to translate. It means something like: jumping suddenly into another situation and being surprised by it, changing your own point of view, and seeing things you thought you knew in a different way."

"Up until two days ago I didn't know my father," I murmur without thinking.

"That's *balikwas*."

Then she tells me other things, and I can't follow every word, but I make an effort, and it seems to me that I get the gist. She says she used to be married, she's twice my age— thirty-seven, to be precise—and then, although the connection escapes me, she says that she and I and everybody are all divided beings: a series of emotions, inclinations and characteristics, desires that pull us in different directions, in contradictory ways, and that we need to squander joy, when it surprises us, because that's the only way not to waste it.

She repeats these words, obviously, they're important, and, in fact, they stay with me: we need to squander joy, that's the only way not to waste it. After all, it disappears afterward anyway.

While we're there, at the kitchen table, on the same side, close to each other, I get this very strange feeling that I don't understand anything and, at the same time, understand everything. Which it then strikes me is precisely the meaning of what she's saying. I think she has a very beautiful face. I like her slightly girlish cheeks. And I like her upper lip—it would be great to be able to draw it. She has a few beads of sweat on that lip, and since I can't draw it, I decide to kiss it, and I do so, and I think that now she'll push me away, she'll call me a child, she'll ask me what got into me, and she'll throw us out, both my father and me, even though he's unaware of what has happened.

This strikes me as an inevitable sequence of events, which I can't do anything to resist. I'm only sorry my father has to undergo this humiliation because of me.

But she doesn't push me away, and her mouth is sweet from the alcohol and the coffee and sour from the cigarette. We kiss, still sitting there, a little twisted. The only sound is the rain, which is still falling, although less than before.

She stands up, takes me by the hand, and leads me to her bedroom. The walls are cream-colored, the bed is the same color, and there's a fresh smell of newly washed sheets.

"I've never made love," I say. You have to be correct in such situations, I think, but she doesn't even reply and makes me sit on the bed. Maybe she places a finger on her mouth to say I have to keep silent. Or maybe I've only imagined that gesture, but the meaning is there: I have to be quiet, I mustn't say anything pointless or stupid. It's only right; we should always avoid saying pointless or stupid things.

At a certain point I'm lying down. She walks away, and comes back and she has something in her hand, and it's the very thing I saw earlier in the medicine cabinet. I whisper to her that I don't know how to put it on, and she says—this time she really does say it, like someone giving orders—that I have to keep quiet.

So she puts it on me, very slowly, very gently and precisely, I don't think I've ever seen a gesture so gentle and so precise, or so kind. Kind is the right word.

You're very kind, Marianne, I'd like to say. But I can't, because of the enormity of what's happening. *Balikwas*—I must remember that—jumping suddenly into another situation.

Jumping.

Suddenly.

Then she takes off her glasses and becomes younger and more fragile.

She gets on top of me, and when we've found a way for me to be inside her, she takes my hands, puts them on her hips, and shows me what to do.

"Slowly, slowly," she whispers. Her French accent is more noticeable, and her breathing becomes labored; it seems to match the rhythm of the water in a gutter outside. She looks at me, and I look at her as she moves until she half closes her eyes and lets out a moan, then another louder one, as if now she's giving me permission.

And it's at this point that we find ourselves together on a steep slope where the whole world spins and plunges and turns upside down and explodes in a Catherine wheel of garish colors.

25

When we walked back into the living room, the Cheshire Cat was alone on the sofa.

My father was outside in the courtyard. He was smoking with his back to us, looking at some vague point beyond the fence. It had stopped raining and everything—the table, the chairs, the plants, the ground—was covered in drops in the semi-darkness. You could sense the end of the night, like an omen. After it, as happened every morning, nothing would be the same.

If Dad was aware of our presence, he didn't let on. He turned slowly—like a character in some films, or in a dream—when I touched his shoulder. All of a sudden, I didn't know what to call him anymore.

"Somebody mentioned coffee," he said with a slight smile. He was pretending everything was normal; only he didn't look like someone pretending that everything is normal. His hair was damp and tidied to the best of his abilities; his face seemed rested.

"I'll go, you two wait here," Marianne replied, also smiling, with a knowingness that sent a shudder through me. For a moment or two, I had the absurd feeling that they had been in cahoots from the start. From before we had left for Marseilles. From long before.

Dad drank his coffee standing in the courtyard, and we too—Marianne and I—stood there, without saying a word, as if we were part of a ceremony, a specific farewell ritual.

Then Marianne walked us to the door. I'd have liked to ask her for her telephone number, to tell her that I wanted to—had to—see her again, but I didn't know how, couldn't find either the words or the courage.

She gave Dad a hug, putting her cheek against his. Then she turned to me and, after a moment's hesitation, stroked my face, and gave me a kiss on the lips, as rapid and light as the touch of a butterfly. Like something that later you don't know if it really happened or if you just imagined it.

The streets of the Panier were deserted and shiny with rain; they seemed to contain all the promises of the future. We got to the Vieux Port just as the huge white clouds were touched with daylight.

The way back was long, much longer than the way there, and when we got to the hotel, dragging our feet by now, the doorman gave us a quizzical look.

We packed our bags, moving in slow motion because of the tiredness, which by now had burst its banks. Every movement—shifting an object, standing up, bending down to pick up a piece of paper from the floor—was an infinite labor. Like moving through a fog wearing wet, heavy clothes. We were silent, because even speaking was too much of an effort.

I still had Marianne's scent on me, faintly, and I wanted to keep it till the last moment. So when the time came to take a final shower in that hotel, I asked my father to go first. He seemed about to reply—there was a risk I might fall asleep and so on—but he must have realized it was no longer necessary. Our journey through those two nights was over.

The taxi dropped us outside the main entrance of the Centre Saint-Paul. We were a few minutes early for our appointment. Dad took out his pack of cigarettes, looked at it, and put it back in his pocket.

He looked like a man about to say goodbye to something.

"Antonio . . ."

"Dad . . ."

"Thanks. It's been a long time since I felt so . . . *awake*. Sometimes the most obvious word is also the most accurate. I've got a desire to do things when we get back. For years I thought I was too old. It's a stupid thing to think, but I only realized that in these past two days."

There are occasions when you need to talk, and you mustn't take anything for granted. Then there are other occasions when you have to keep silent because there's something intangible, something precious in the air, and your words might dispel it in an instant.

These are two simple concepts. The hard part is to know when to apply one rule and when the other.

This time, there was nothing to say. I had to let him speak, and it didn't take much to realize that. Two nights without sleep weaken you, slow down your reflexes, blur your vision, but they give you a very subtle, precise sense of what really matters.

"And you're going to be fine, that's the most important thing," he said at last.

Then he gave me a pat—almost a caress—on the cheek and headed for the main entrance of the center.

26

I was cured, the professor said.

Then he repeated word for word the sentence he'd used two days earlier, which seemed like ten years earlier, a whole lifetime earlier: I could forget about hospitals, EEGs, barbiturates, and, above all, neurologists. I don't know if he did it deliberately, to show how well he remembered his own words, or if that was the formula he always recited when announcing that a patient was cured.

As if my mind were on a roller coaster, I felt two diametrically opposed emotions, one after the other.

At first, I was overcome with euphoria.

I was going to be a normal young man again, without any secret, shameful handicap, without any mortgage on my future, without any rules about what I could and couldn't do—without the need to keep telling myself that everything was fine, even though I knew perfectly well that everything wasn't fine as long as I needed medicine.

Then the euphoria faded and gave way to dismay.

In all those years, the pill, its ritual, and what surrounded it had been perfect alibis for avoiding any responsibility and even feeling that I didn't owe life anything. Now, all at once, the alibis were gone: they had been wiped out with a nod of the head and a few words spoken in a French accent.

All at once, I found myself out at sea, and I wasn't ready.

But is anyone ever ready?

After that, we slept.

We slept in the taxi taking us to the airport; we slept at the departure gate, once we'd gotten through the formalities and passed the controls; we slept deeply on the plane, for the whole duration of the flight, until a few minutes before landing.

Dad saw me home in a taxi. We were awake again, and quite rested, but an awkward silence had fallen between us. After so much unexpected intimacy, we were back in the familiar places, where habit was already, insidiously, trying to regain the upper hand.

He told the driver to wait for him and got out with me. The taxi had stopped a few meters from the front door of the building. I took my suitcase from the trunk and stood there, as if undecided. But I knew perfectly well what to do.

I put my suitcase down on the ground and hugged my father; the last time I'd done that, I was nine years old. He gave off a slight smell of eau de cologne and cigarettes—the smell of a man of the past.

Before going into the entrance hall, I turned to look. He raised his arm; unusually, he wasn't smoking.

I saw him other times after that, of course. But when I remember him without thinking of a specific situation, or when sometimes I dream of him, Dad is there, by that taxi, slightly disorientated, waving to me. And we stay like that for a few seconds—or a few hours—before I wake up.

Epilogue

It was April, ten months later, when Dad finished his teaching lesson, left the classroom, and told the janitor that he wasn't feeling well and might need a doctor. The janitor made him sit down, loosened his tie, and, worried by now, ran to get help. By the time he got back, to say that an ambulance had arrived, it was already all over.

It was my mother who gave me the letter, along with other things found in Dad's desk. Her eyes were watery, and she seemed lost in a way I'd never seen before.

The handwriting was clear and readable, full of sharp points, but also of sudden soft curves. Beautiful, clear, and straight, even though the paper was unlined. Just one page, light and almost cheerful. It wasn't folded, and there was no envelope: it hadn't been written to be sent.

He was glad, Dad said, of the unexpected, unforeseeable opportunity that we'd had in Marseilles; the things we'd said to each other and the things that had remained un-said, because they were a reason to talk some more. And we would; there was no hurry, we just had to find the right opportunity.

That's what I'd thought too, in the days and months following our trip. We would talk again. We had time.

I've just turned fifty-one, the age my father was back then. If Dad were still here, he'd be eighty-four. It's strange, thinking of him as an old man. To be honest, however hard I try, I can't quite manage it.

Mom is eighty-one, still a strong woman, still beautiful. The only sign that she's getting old is that she's increasingly inclined to tell stories about the distant past. In a lot of these stories, she and my father are children.

Marianne was thirty-seven, and always will be. I don't know anything about her, not even if she's still alive. All I know is that her apartment was in Rue du Refuge, in the old neighborhood of the Panier, in Marseilles.

My father's letter to me ended with a quotation from the great mathematician John von Neumann: "If people do not believe that mathematics is simple, it is only because they do not realize how complicated life is."

I've copied it onto the wall of my office at the university.

Maybe that's all there is to know.

A Note from the Translator

Gianrico Carofiglio is a writer preoccupied with language, with how it is used and how it should be used. In parallel to his output of novels—notably the series of legal thrillers featuring defense lawyer Guido Guerrieri that has made his fame in Italy and around the world—he has produced a number of book-length essays examining, among other things, how words can be misused to manipulate and distort the truth, especially in the law and politics. (He knows whereof he speaks, having been both a public prosecutor and a senator in the Italian parliament.) He is a champion of clarity in language, and his own prose, in both fiction and nonfiction, is direct, limpid, and unambiguous.

It is tempting for translators to tell heroic stories of how they have struggled with complex language, erudite metaphors, twisted syntax, fiendish plays on words—none of this with Carofiglio. Having now translated eight of his novels, I can report that the translator's task, where this writer is concerned, is actively to avoid introducing unnecessary complexity and ambiguity to the texts and to precisely match originals that are deliberately stripped-down, plain-speaking, and, above all, communicative.

This is basically a novel about communication, a story of a father and son who, through extraordinary circumstances, are forced to spend time together and, in doing so, to discover truths about each other they might not otherwise have learned. They do this mainly by talking, really talking to each other, for the first time in their lives. In the Guerrieri series, the lawyer-hero often has to cut through the obfuscations of legal jargon to get at the truth of a case; here, the characters, over the course of two sleepless days and nights in Marseilles, discover the power of words to reveal the truth of the human soul. And it is the power of Carofiglio's words that I hope I, as a translator, have conveyed.

—Howard Curtis

Here ends Gianrico Carofiglio's
Three O'Clock in the Morning.

The first edition of this book was printed
and bound at LSC Communications in
Harrisonburg, Virginia, in 2021.

A NOTE ON THE TYPE

The text of this novel was set in Granjon, an old-style serif typeface designed by George W. Jones for Linotype in 1928. Considered one of many Garamond revivals created in the 1920s, Granjon actually takes its name from the type designer Robert Granjon, another key influence. Graceful and readable, it continues to be a popular choice for print.

HarperVia

An imprint dedicated to publishing international voices,
offering readers a chance to encounter other lives and other
points of view via the language of the imagination.